'I want my son to grow up in Spain—'

'Well, you can't always have what you want,' Jemima pointed out flatly.

Alejandro strolled across the floor towards her. 'I gave this matter serious thought last night. I can give you a choice…'

Her spine went rigid, her eyes flying wide with uncertainty. 'What sort of a choice?'

'Option one: you return to Spain and give our marriage another chance. Or option two: I take you to court over Alfie and we fight for him.' As Jemima lost colour and a look of disbelief tautened her delicate pointed features, Alejandro surveyed her with unblemished cool. 'From my point of view it's a very fair offer, and more than you deserve.'

SECRETLY PREGNANT

With this ring, I claim my baby!

The amazing new trilogy
by best-selling Modern™ Romance author

Lynne Graham

The charming and pretty English village of
Charlbury St Helens is home to three young women
whose Cinderella lives are about to be turned upside
down…by three of the wealthiest, most handsome and
impossibly arrogant men in Europe!

Jemima, Flora and Jess aren't looking for love,
but all have babies very much in mind.
Jemima already has a young son,
Flora is hoping to adopt her late half-sister's
little daughter, and Jess just longs to be a mum.

But whether they have or want a baby,
all the girls must marry ultimate alpha males
to keep their dreams… And Alejandro,
Angelo and Cesario are not about to be tamed!

SECRETLY PREGNANT

NAÏVE BRIDE, DEFIANT WIFE:
Jemima and Alejandro's story

FLORA'S DEFIANCE:
Flora and Angelo's story

JESS'S PROMISE:
Jess and Cesario's story

NAÏVE WIFE, DEFIANT BRIDE

BY
LYNNE GRAHAM

All the characters in this book have no existence outside the imagination of the author, and have no relation whatsoever to anyone bearing the same name or names. They are not even distantly inspired by any individual known or unknown to the author, and all the incidents are pure invention.

First published in Great Britain 2010
Harlequin Mills & Boon Limited,
Eton House, 18-24 Paradise Road, Richmond, Surrey TW9 1SR

© Lynne Graham 2010

ISBN: 978 0 263 87863 9

Harlequin Mills & Boon policy is to use papers that are natural, renewable and recyclable products and made from wood grown in sustainable forests. The logging and manufacturing process conform to the legal environmental regulations of the country of origin.

Printed and bound in Spain
by Litografia Rosés, S.A., Barcelona

NAÏVE WIFE, DEFIANT BRIDE

CHAPTER ONE

ALEJANDRO NAVARRO VASQUEZ, the Conde Olivares, sat on his superb black stallion in the shade of an orange grove and surveyed the valley that had belonged to his ancestors for over five hundred years. On this fine spring morning, below a clear blue sky, it was a gorgeous view encompassing thousands of acres of fertile earth and woodland. He owned the land as far as the eye could see, but his lean, darkly handsome features were grim as they had often been since the breakdown of his marriage almost two and a half years earlier.

He was a landowner and wealthy, but his family—which every Spaniard cherished far beyond material riches—had been ripped asunder by his imprudent marriage. For a male as strong, proud and successful as Alejandro, it was a bitter truth that undermined his every achievement. He had followed his heart and not his head and he had married the wrong woman, a very expensive mistake for which he was still paying the price. His half-brother, Marco, had taken a job in New York, cutting off all contact with his mother and siblings. Yet if Marco, whom Alejandro had helped to raise after their father's premature death, had appeared before him at that moment could he have forgiven the younger man and urged him back to his childhood home with sincerity and warm affection?

Alejandro swore under his breath as he pondered that merciless question and the less than acceptable negative answer that he would have had to give it. However, when it came to *Jemima*, there was no forgiveness in his heart, only outrage and aggression. He nursed a far from charitable desire for vengeance against the wife and the brother who had together betrayed his trust and his love. Ever since Jemima had walked out on their marriage and disappeared, defying his wishes to the last, Alejandro had burned with a desire for justice, even while his keen intelligence warned him that there was no such thing when it came to affairs of the heart.

His mobile phone vibrated and, suppressing a groan of impatience, for it was always a struggle to protect his rare moments of leisure, he tugged it out. His ebony brows rose when he learned that the private detective he had hired to find Jemima had arrived to see him. He rode swiftly back to the castle, wondering impatiently if Alonso Ortega had finally managed to track down his estranged wife.

'My apologies for coming to see you without an appointment, Your Excellency,' the older man murmured with punctilious good manners and a promising air of accomplishment. 'But I knew you would want to hear my news as soon as possible. I have found the Condesa.'

'In England?' Alejandro questioned and, having had that long-held suspicion confirmed, he listened while Ortega furnished further details. Then, unfortunately, at that point his mother, the dowager countess, entered the room. A formidable presence, Doña Hortencia settled acid black eyes on the private detective and demanded to know if he had finally fulfilled the purpose of his hire. At the news that he had, a rare smile of approval lightened her expression.

'There is one more fact I should add,' Ortega revealed in a reluctant tone of voice, evading the uncomfortably intense scrutiny of his noble hostess. 'The Condesa now has a child, a little boy of around two years of age.'

Alejandro froze and a yawning silence greeted the detective's startling announcement.

The door opened again and his older sister, Beatriz, entered with a quiet apology to her brother for the interruption. She was hushed into silence by her domineering mother, who said glacially, 'That wanton English witch who married your unlucky brother has given birth to a bastard.'

Horrified at such an announcement being made in front of Alonso Ortega, Beatriz shot her brother an appalled glance and hastened to offer the detective refreshments in an effort to change the subject to one less controversial. His discomfited sister, Alejandro appreciated, would quite happily sit and discuss the weather now while he, her more primitive brother, was strongly tempted to seize hold of Ortega's lapels and force every single fact from the man without further ado. But, possibly sensing his employer's impatience, the detective handed Alejandro a slim file and hastily excused himself.

'A…child?' Beatriz gasped in shock and consternation the instant the door had closed on the detective's departure. 'But *whose* child?'

His profile set like granite, Alejandro answered his sister only with a dismissive shrug. It was certainly not his child, but for him that had to be the biggest badge of ignominy he had ever endured. Yet another metaphorical nail in Jemima's coffin, he conceded bitterly. Jemima, he had learned the hard way, knew exactly how best to put a man through an emotional and physical wringer. *Dios mio*, another man's child!

'If only you had listened to me,' Doña Hortencia lamented. 'The instant I met that wicked young woman I knew she was wrong for you. You were one of the biggest matrimonial prizes in Spain and you could have married anyone—'

'I married Jemima,' Alejandro pointed out tersely, for he had never had much time for the older woman's melodrama.

'Only because she mesmerised you like the shameless hussy she is. One man was never going to be enough for her. Thanks to her, my poor Marco is living on the other side of the world. That she could have given birth to an illegitimate child while still bearing our name is the most disgusting thing I ever—'

'Enough!' Alejandro incised with crushing force to close out that carping voice. 'There is no point to such recriminations now. What is done is done.'

Doña Hortencia, her lined face full of anger and malice, rested accusing eyes on his lean strong visage. 'But it is *not* done yet, is it? You still haven't begun divorce proceedings.'

'I will travel to England and see Jemima as soon as the arrangements can be made,' Alejandro pronounced grittily.

'Send the family lawyer! There can be no need for you to make a personal trip to England,' his mother protested with vigour.

'There is every need,' Alejandro contradicted with all

the quiet, unhesitating assurance of his rich, well-educated and extremely aristocratic background. 'Jemima is still my wife.'

As Doña Hortencia broke into another barrage of loud objections Alejandro lost patience. 'I inform you of my intentions only as a matter of courtesy. I do not require either your permission or your approval.'

Alejandro retired to the privacy of his study and poured himself a stiff brandy. A child? Jemima had had a child. He was still in shock at that revelation, not least because he could hardly forget that his wife had miscarried *his* baby shortly before she'd left him. That was how he knew beyond any shadow of doubt that this child, which she had given birth to since, then could not possibly be his. So, was the boy Marco's baby? Or some other man's? Such speculation was sordid, he acknowledged with a distaste that slivered through his lean powerful frame like a knife blade.

He leafed through the file but the facts were few. Jemima was now living in a Dorset village where she ran a florist's shop. For a moment as he allowed himself to think about his estranged wife memories threatened to overwhelm him, but he shut them out, utilising the fierce intelligence and self-discipline that were second nature to him. Yet where had either trait been when he got involved with Jemima Grey in the first place?

He could make no excuses for his behaviour because he had freely acknowledged the huge and irrefutable differences between them even before he married her. Of course, what had mesmerised him then—to borrow his mother's expression—was Jemima's superlative sex appeal. Like many men, he had been more vulnerable to that temptation than he had ever realised he might be.

Possibly life prior to that point had spoiled him with too many easy female conquests. His failure to keep a lid on his fierce sexual desire to possess Jemima's pale slim body had proved to be his fatal weakness, he assured himself with grim conviction. Fortunately, however, the passage of time and the process of hard disillusionment he had experienced during his short-lived marriage had obliterated Jemima's desirability factor entirely.

His ill-judged marriage had, after all, virtually destroyed his family circle. But in the short term, Jemima had no family support of her own and she was still his legal wife; regardless of his feelings on that score she remained *his* responsibility. As did her child, whom the law would deem to be his child until a divorce was finalised, Alejandro conceded, irate at that demeaning fact. He had to go to England.

No Conde Olivares since the fifteenth century had ever been known to act as a coward or to shirk his duty, no matter how unpleasant it might be. Even in the most trying circumstances, Alejandro expected no less of himself. He reckoned that Jemima was fortunate to be a twenty-first-century woman, for his medieval ancestors would have locked an unfaithful wife up in a convent or killed her for inflicting such a stain on the family honour. Though at least his less civilised ancestors had possessed the power of retaliation, he reflected broodingly.

While Jemima wrapped the bouquet in clear, decorative cellophane, Alfie peered round the corner of the shop counter, his big brown eyes dancing with mischief. "'Ello,' he said chirpily to the waiting customer, shyness not being one of Alfie's personality traits.

'Hello. He's a beautiful child,' the woman remarked, smiling down at Alfie as the toddler looked up at her with his irrepressible grin.

It was a compliment that often came Alfie's way, his mother conceded as she slotted the payment in the till, while wondering what age her son would reach before that particular description embarrassed him. But like father like son, she thought ruefully, and in looks Alfie was very much a product of his Spanish father's genes, with gorgeous dark brown eyes, olive-tinted skin and a shock of black silky hair. All he had inherited from his less exotic mother was her rampant curls. On the inside, however, Alfie had all the easy warmth of his mother's essentially optimistic nature and revealed only the occasional hint of his father's infinitely darker and more passionate temperament.

With a slight shiver, Jemima pushed that daunting thought back out of her mind again. With Alfie playing with his toy cars at her feet, she returned to fashioning a flower arrangement requested by a client who had photographed a similar piece of floral art at a horticultural show. Pure accident had brought Jemima to the village of Charlbury St Helens at a crisis point in her life and she had never regretted staying on and laying the foundations for her new future there.

The only work she'd been able to find locally while she'd been pregnant was as an assistant at a flower shop. She had needed to earn back her self-respect by keeping busy and positive. Discovering that she had a very real interest in floristry, she had found more than a job to focus on and had since studied part-time for formal qualifications. By the time her employer decided to retire, owing to ill health, Jemima had had the courage and vision to take over the business and expand it by taking on occasional private projects that encompassed small weddings and other functions.

She was so proud of running her own business that sometimes she had to pinch herself to believe that she could have come so far from her humble beginnings. Not bad for the daughter of a violent, criminal father who had never worked if he could help it, and a downtrodden, alcoholic mother, who had died when her husband crashed a stolen car. Jemima had never dared to develop any aspirations as a teenager. Nobody in her family tree had ever tried to climb the career or social ladders.

'Those kinds of ideas aren't for the likes of us. Jem needs to get a job to help out at home,' her mother had told the teacher who'd tried to persuade the older woman that her daughter should stay on at school to study for her A-level exams.

'You're like your mother—dumb as a rock and just about as useful!' her father had condemned often enough for that label to have troubled Jemima for many year afterwards.

With lunch eaten, she walked Alfie down to his session at the playgroup in the village hall, wincing when her son bounded boisterously through the door calling his friends' names at the top of his voice. Alfie, named for his great-grandfather on Jemima`s mother's side of the family, was very sociable and full of energy after spending the morning cooped up at the shop with his mother. Although Jemima had created a play corner in the backstore room for her child, there really wasn't enough space to house a lively little boy for long. With the help of a childminder, she had often contrived to keep Alfie with her during working hours, but now that he was of an age to join the playgroup in the afternoons and she no longer attended floristry classes she needed a lot less childcare. Considering that her close friend and former childminder, Flora, was now often too busy with her bed-and- breakfast operation to help out as much, Jemima was grateful for that fact.

It was a pleasant surprise therefore when Flora came into the shop an hour later and asked Jemima if she had time for a coffee. Brewing up in the small kitchen, Jemima eyed her red-headed friend and read the other woman's uneasiness with a frown. 'What's up?'

'It's probably nothing. I meant to come over and tell you at the weekend, but a whole family booked in with me on Saturday and I was run off my feet,' Flora groaned. 'Apparently some guy in a hire car was hanging around the village last Thursday and someone saw him taking a picture of your shop. He was asking questions about you in the post office as well.'

Jemima stilled, dark blue eyes widening while her heart-shaped face paled below her cloud of wildly curling strawberry-blonde hair and the stance of her tiny slender figure screamed tension. Just an inch over five feet in height, she had reminded the more solidly built Flora of a delicate blown-glass angel ornament when they'd first met, but she had later appreciated that nobody as down-to-earth and quirky as Jemima could be seen for long in that improbable light. However, her friend was unquestionably beautiful in an ethereal way and if men could be equated to starving dogs, Jemima was the equivalent of a very juicy bone, for the male sex seemed to find her irresistible. Locals joked that the church choir had been on the brink of folding before Jemima had joined and a swell of young men had soon followed in her wake, not that any of them had since got anywhere with her, Flora reflected wryly. Badly burned by her failed marriage, Jemima preferred men as friends and concentrated her energies on her son and her business.

'What sort of questions?' Jemima prompted sickly, the cold chill of apprehension hollowing out her stomach.

'Whether or not you lived around here, and what age Alfie was. The guy asking the questions was young and good-looking. Maurice in the post office thought he was playing cupid...'

'Was the man Spanish?'

Flora shook her head and took over from her anxious friend at the kettle to speed up the arrival of the coffee. 'No, a Londoner according to Maurice. He probably just fancied trying his chances with you—'

'I don't remember *any* young good-looking men coming in here last week,' Jemima pointed out, her concern patent.

'Maybe he lost interest once he realised you were a mother.' Flora shrugged. 'I wouldn't have told you about him if I had known you would get wound up about it. Why don't you just get on the phone and tell...er...what's his name, your husband?'

'Alejandro,' Jemima supplied tautly. 'Tell him what?'

'That you want a clean break and a divorce.'

'Nobody gets away with telling Alejandro what to do. He's the one who does the telling. It wouldn't be that simple once he found out about Alfie.'

'So you go to a solicitor and say what a lousy husband he was.'

'He didn't drink or beat me up.'

Flora grimaced. 'Why should such extremes be your

only yardstick? There are other grounds for divorce, like mental abuse and neglect—and what about the way he left you at the mercy of his horrible family?'

'It was his mother who was horrible, not his brother or his sister,' Jemima pointed out, wanting as always to be fair. 'And I don't think it's right to say I was mentally abused.'

Flora, whose temper was as hot as her hair, regarded the younger woman with unimpressed eyes. 'Alejandro criticised everything you did, left you alone all the time and got you pregnant before you were ready to have a kid.'

Jemima reddened to the roots of her light-coloured hair and marvelled that she could have been so frank with Flora in the early weeks of their friendship, sharing secrets that she sometimes wished she had kept to herself, although not, mercifully, the worst secrets of all. Of course, back then, she had been as steamed up as a pressure cooker of emotions and in dire need of someone to talk to. 'I just wasn't good enough for him...' She spoke the truth as she saw it, as lightly as she could.

Growing up, Jemima had never been good enough for either of her parents and the ability to search out and focus on her own flaws was second nature to her. Her mother had entered her in juvenile beauty contests as a young child but Jemima, too shy to smile for the photos and too quiet to chatter when interviewed, had not shone. Bored out of her mind as she was as a daydreaming teenager, she had done equally poorly at the office-skills course her mother had sent her on, shattering her mother's second dream of her becoming a high-powered personal assistant to some millionaire who would some day fall madly in love with her daughter. Her mother had pretty much lived in a fantasy world, which, along with the alcohol, had provided her with her only escape from the drudgery and abuse of a bad marriage.

Jemima's father, whose only dreams related to making pots of money without ever getting up off the sofa, had wanted Jemima to become a model, but she failed to grow tall enough for fashion work and lacked the bountiful curves necessary for the other kind. After her mother's death, her father had urged her to become a dancer at a club run by his mate and had hit her and thrown her out of the family home when she'd refused to dress up in a skimpy outfit and attend an audition. It was years before she saw her father again and then in circumstances she preferred to forget. Yes, Jemima had learned at an early age that people always expected more from her than she ever seemed able to deliver and, sadly, her marriage had proved no different. It was for that reason that making her own way in life to set up and run her business had added greatly to her confidence; for once she had surpassed her own expectations.

Yet when she had first met Alejandro and he had swept her off her feet, he had seemed to be *her* every dream come true, which in retrospect seemed laughable to her. But love had snatched her up like a tornado and made her believe in the impossible before it flung her down again. Somehow, and she had no idea how, she had truly believed that she could marry a rich, educated foreigner with a pedigree as long as her arm and make a go of it. But in practice the challenges and the disparities had proved insurmountable. Her background had come back to seriously haunt her, but her biggest single mistake had been getting too friendly with her brother-in-law, Marco. Although, she reasoned defensively, had

Alejandro been around more and made more effort to help her come to terms with her new life in Spain she wouldn't have been so lonely and wouldn't have jumped at the offer of Marco's company. And she had *adored* Marco, she acknowledged abstractedly, recalling how wounded she had felt when even after her marriage broke down he had made no attempt to get in touch with her again.

'You were *too* good for that husband of yours,' Flora told Jemima with strong emphasis. 'But you really should tell Alejandro about Alfie instead of staying in hiding as if you have something to be ashamed of.'

Jemima turned her head away, her cheeks colouring as she thought, *If only you knew...* Telling the whole unvarnished truth would probably turn her closest friend off her as well, she reckoned painfully.

'I honestly believe that if Alejandro found out about Alfie, he would go to any lengths to get custody of him and take him back to Spain to live,' she replied heavily. 'Alejandro takes his responsibilities towards the family very seriously.'

'Well, if you think there's a risk of Alfie being snatched by his father, you're wise keeping quiet about him,' Flora said, although there was an uncertain look on her face when she voiced that opinion. 'But you can't keep him quiet for ever.'

'Only, for now, it's the best option,' Jemima declared, setting down her coffee to attend to a customer as the shop bell on the door sounded.

Soon afterwards, she went out to deliver a floral arrangement for a dinner party to one of the big houses outside the village. On the way home she collected Alfie, his high energy dissipated by a couple of hours of horseplay. The tiny terraced cottage she rented on the outskirts of the village enjoyed a garden, which she had equipped with a swing and a sandpit. She was proud of her small living space. Although the little house was inexpertly painted and furnished cheaply with flat-pack furniture, it was the first place she had ever been able to make feel like her home since childhood.

Sometimes it seemed like a dim and unbelievable fairy tale to recall that after she had married Alejandro she had lived in a castle. *Castillo del Halcón*, the Castle of the Hawk, built by his warrior ancestors in a mix of Islamic and European styles and filled with history, luxury and priceless artefacts. Moving the furniture or the pictures around had been forbidden and redecorating equally frowned on because the dowager countess, Doña Hortencia, could not bear any woman to interfere in what she still essentially saw as her home. Living there, Jemima had often felt like a lodger who had outstayed her welcome, and the formal lifestyle of changing into evening clothes for dinner, dealing with servants and entertaining important guests had suited her even less.

Had there been any redeeming features to her miserable marriage? she asked herself, and instantly a picture of Alejandro popped up unbidden inside her head. Her spectacularly gorgeous husband had initially felt like a prize beyond any other she had ever received, yet she had never quite been able to stifle the feeling that she didn't deserve him and he deserved better than her. It crossed Jemima's mind that most of the best things that had happened to her in life had occurred seemingly because of blessed accidents of fate. That description best covered Alfie's unplanned conception, her car choosing to break down in Charlbury St Helens after she had run away from Spain, her marriage, and ironically it even covered her first meeting with Alejandro...

He had knocked her off her bike in a car park or, rather, his driver's overly assertive driving style had done so. She had been on her day off from the hotel where she was working as a receptionist and riding a bicycle was a necessity when she was employed in a rural business and buses were scarcer than hens' teeth. The opulent Mercedes had ground to a halt and Alejandro and his chauffeur had emerged to check out the damage done while she was struggling to blink back tears from the pain of her skinned knees and bruised hip. Before she had known what was happening to her, her damaged bike was stacked in the local repair shop and she was ensconced in the luxury Mercedes, being swept off to the nearest hospital A and E department by the most gorgeous-looking guy she had ever met in her life. It was a shame that she really hadn't noticed that day just how domineering and deaf to all argument Alejandro could be, for he had refused to listen when she declared that she did not require any medical attention. No, she had been X-rayed, cleaned up, bandaged and bullied within an inch of her life all because Alejandro's dazzling smile had cast a spell over her.

Love at first sight, Jemima labelled with an instinctive frown of antipathy while she shifted about restlessly in her bed that night. She had never believed in love at first sight, indeed had grown up promising herself that she would never allow any man to wield the kind of power over her that her father had always exercised over her mother. But despite the hard lessons she had believed she had learned at her mother's knee, Jemima had taken one look at Alejandro Navarro Vasquez and fallen as hard and as destructively for him as a brick thrown from a major height. And the *real* lessons she had learned she had picked up from Alejandro himself, only she had failed to put what she learned to sensible use.

Long before Alejandro had shocked her with his proposal of marriage, he had put her through months of dating hell by not phoning when he said he would, by cancelling meetings last minute and by seeing other women and getting photographed with them. Even before she'd married him he had battered her heart and trodden her pride deep in the dirt. But she had understood even then why he was giving her the runaround. He was, after all, a Spanish count, while she worked for peanuts at a little hotel that he considered to be a dump. He had known she was not his equal on any level and the disparity had bothered him deeply from the outset of their acquaintance. Six months after that first encounter, however, Alejandro had seemed to shed that attitude…

'*Sol y sombre*…sun and shade, *querida mia*,' Alejandro had murmured then as he compared the pale skin of her slender arm to the bronzed vibrancy of his darker colouring. 'You cannot have one without the other—we belong together.'

But they had mingled as badly as oil and water, Jemima conceded with the dulled pain of acceptance that she had learned she had to live with, and she finally dropped off to sleep around two in the morning by dint of trying to forget the delivery she had to get up for the next morning.

There was hardly any floor space left in the shop once

she had loaded the fresh blooms into the waiting containers. Her fingers numbed by the brisk spring morning temperature and too much contact with wet stems and water, Jemima rubbed her hands over her slim jeans-clad hips and tried not to shiver, because she knew that one shiver would only lead to another half-dozen and that in the end she would only feel colder. After all, winter or summer, the shop was always cool. It was an old building with poor insulation and she was always quick to remind herself that too much heat would only damage her stock. She went into the back room and dragged a black fleece jacket off the hook in the wall and put it on. Alfie was out in the little backyard playing on his trike while making loud motoring noises and she smiled at the sight of his innocent enjoyment, which took no account of the early hour he had been dug out of his cosy bed or the chilly air.

'Jemima…'

It was a voice she had hoped never to hear again: rich, melodic, dark and deep, and so full of accented earthy male sexiness it sent little quivers down her sensitive spine. She shut her eyes tight, refusing to turn round, telling herself wildly that her mind had somehow slipped dangerously back into the past and that she was imagining things…

Imagining waking up in bed with Alejandro, all tousled black hair, stubble and raw male sensual appeal… Alejandro, who could ignite her hunger with one indolent glance from his stunning black-fringed dark-as-the-night-sky eyes and seal it by simply saying her name… But even as a steamy burst of imagery momentarily clouded her brain and interfered with her breathing, she was instead recalling the emptiness of her bed once she had fallen pregnant and the wounding anguish of that physical lack of interest in her rapidly swelling body. As a chill slid through her slender length she spun round.

And there he was, Alejandro Navarro Vasquez, her husband, who had taught her to love him, taught her to need him and who had then proceeded to torture her with deprivation for her weakness. She was shocked, deeply, horribly shocked, her dazed violet-blue eyes widening to roam slowly over him as if she could not credit what she was seeing. Thick blue-black hair swept back from his brow, a fitting overture to the splendour of high patrician cheekbones bisected by a strong arrogant nose and punctuated by a sensually shaped and perfect masculine mouth. He was a staggeringly handsome man and fabulously well turned out in a dark business suit of faultless cut and polished handmade shoes. He always looked immaculate…except in bed, she recalled dully, when her hands had disarranged his hair and her nails had inflicted scratch marks down the long golden expanse of his flawless back. And she wanted to scream against the recollections that would not leave her alone, that were uniting with her sense of panic to destabilise her even more.

'What are you doing here?' she exclaimed breathlessly…

CHAPTER TWO

'WE HAVE unfinished business,' Alejandro intoned softly, his keen gaze wandering slowly over her small figure.

And Jemima went from cold to hot as if he had turned a blowtorch on her. She flushed because she knew she looked less than her best with her hair loose round her to keep her ears warm and only a touch of mascara and lip gloss on her face, not to mention the worn jeans, fleece jacket and shabby low-heeled boots that completed her practical outfit. And even though it was bloody-minded—for she wanted nothing between them to be as it had once been, when she'd had no control over her responses—she deeply resented his cool stare and businesslike tone: it was the ultimate rejection. She leant against the door frame, her slender spine taking on an arch that enhanced the small firm curves below the neat fit of wool and denim, her head lifting so that the pale foaming ringlets of her eye-catching strawberry-blonde hair rippled back across her shoulders.

An almost infinitesimal tightening hardened Alejandro's darkly handsome features, his sculpted jaw line clenching, his brilliant gaze narrowing and bright-ening. Then Jemima knew he had felt the challenge from her as stridently and clearly as though she had used a loud hailer. Suddenly the atmosphere was seething with tension. At that point, she suffered a dismaying reduction in courage and veiled her gaze, drawing back a step while being terrifyingly aware of the swelling tightness of her nipples inside her bra and the twisting slide of sexual awareness low in her pelvis. It shocked her that a man she now hated as much as she had once loved him could still have such a powerful effect on her body.

'Always the temptress,' Alejandro drawled with a roughened edge to his dark deep voice that vibrated through her like a jamming wireless signal and made her rigidity give way to a trembling vulnerability. 'Do I really look that desperate?'

The fierce chill of his rejection might have cut her like a knife had she not been more aware of the way his strikingly beautiful eyes lingered on her. As she tore her attention from the lean, strong face that haunted her dreams and her gaze dropped she could not help noticing the distinctive masculine bulge that had disturbed the perfect fit of his trousers. Her cheeks flamed as hot as a kettle on the boil as she was both mollified by that reaction and burned by it at the same time.

'What are you doing here?' she demanded for the second time.

'I want a divorce. I need an address for you to obtain it,' Alejandro spelt out in a driven undertone. 'Or didn't that occur to you? Your staging a vanishing act was selfish and immature.'

That fast Jemima wanted to lift one of the buckets of flowers and upend it over him. 'You forced me to behave like that,' she told him heatedly.

'How?' Alejandro growled, striding forward to brace

his lean, well-shaped hands on the counter, clearly more than ready for an argument.

'You wouldn't listen to a word I said. We had reached stalemate and there was nothing more I could do.'

'I told you that we would work it out,' Alejandro reminded her in a tone of galling condescension.

'But in the whole of our marriage you never did work anything out with me. How could you when you wouldn't talk to me? When I told you how unhappy I was what did you ever do to make anything better?' Jemima demanded, her violet eyes shimmering with pain and condemnation as she remembered the lavish gifts he had given her instead of more concrete and meaningful things like his time and his attention.

Straight away, anger flared in Alejandro, his stunning eyes flaming bright gold with heat just as the bell on the shop door rang to herald the arrival of Jemima's assistant, Sandy. The silence inside the shop was so deep and so tense it could have filled a bank vault and as she came in the dark-haired, neatly dressed older woman shot Jemima a look of dismay. 'Am I late? Were you expecting me to start early today?'

'No, no,' Jemima hastened to reassure her employee. 'But I'm afraid I have to go back home for an hour, so you'll be in charge.'

Without even looking in Alejandro's direction, Jemima went out to the backyard to retrieve Alfie, hoisting him into her arms and hurrying back indoors to say in a frazzled aside to Alejandro, 'I live a hundred yards down the road at number forty-two.'

But before she could reach the door a broad-shouldered young man with cropped fair hair strolled through it brandishing a bag. 'Fresh out of the bakery oven,

Jemima!' he exclaimed with satisfaction. 'Cherry scones
for our elevenses...'

'Oh, Charlie, I totally forgot you were coming today!'
Jemima gasped in dismay. She had made the arrangement the previous week when she'd last seen Charlie at
choir practice. 'Look, I have to go out for a little while,
but first I'd better show you that electrical socket that's
not working.'

Anchoring Alfie more firmly to her hip, Jemima
dived back behind the counter with Charlie close behind
her and pointed out the socket that had failed the previous week.

Full of cheerful chatter, Charlie rested appreciative
eyes on her delicate profile. 'If it would suit you better
I can come back tomorrow when you're here.'

'No, that's fine, Charlie. Today is perfect,' Jemima
insisted, turning back to head for the door where
Alejandro waited in silence, his shrewd gaze pinned to
the hovering electrician, who was making no attempt
to hide his disappointment that she was leaving. 'Sandy
will look after you.'

Jemima stepped out into the fresh air, hugely conscious of Alejandro's presence by her side but also per-
plexed, because if he had even looked at Alfie for ten
seconds he had contrived to hide the fact from her. 'I'll
see you at the house,' she said flatly, setting Alfie down
and grasping his hand because he was too heavy for her
to carry any further.

'I'll give you a lift,' Alejandro drawled.

'No, thanks.' Without any further ado, Jemima
crossed the road and began to walk away fast with Alfie
tottering along beside her. Outside working hours she

used the van to get around, but when the shop was open it was needed to deliver orders.

She had only gone twenty yards before a neat, dark saloon car pulled in beside her and the driver's door opened. Then a tall man in a business suit climbed out. 'Going home?' Jeremy prompted. 'Get in. I'll drop you off.'

'Thank you, Jeremy, but I'm so close it's easier just to walk,' she declared breezily, though all her thoughts were miles away, lodged back on Alejandro and his assurance that he wanted a divorce.

Had he already met someone else? Some well born beauty from a moneyed background, much more suitable than she had been? She wondered how many other women he had been with since she had left him and it made a tiny shudder of agonising emotional pain arrow through her tender heart. She didn't want Alejandro back, no, she definitely didn't, but she didn't want any other woman to have him either. Where he was concerned, she was a real dog in the manger. But it would be foolish to imagine that he might have been celibate since her departure, for that high-voltage libido of his required frequent gratification…or at least it had until he was faced with her enlarged breasts and thickening waistline and it had become painfully, hurtfully obvious that he'd found his pregnant wife's body about as attractive as a mud bath. So how could she possibly care what he had done and with whom since then?

Jeremy yanked open the passenger door of his car. 'Get in,' he urged. 'You're both getting soaked.'

Belatedly appreciating that it had started raining while she'd stood there, Jemima scooped up her son and clambered in. Jeremy pulled in just ahead of the

sleek sports car already waiting outside her home. He
vented a low whistle of appreciation as he studied the
opulent model. 'Who on earth does that beauty belong
to?'

'An old friend of mine,' she replied as she stepped
out of his car. 'Thanks.'

As she attempted to turn away Jeremy strode round
the bonnet to rest a staying hand on her arm. 'Eat out
with me tonight,' he urged, his blue eyes pinned hope-
fully to her face. 'No strings, no big deal, just a couple
of friends getting together for a meal.'

Turning pink, Jemima stepped back from his proxim-
ity, awesomely conscious that just feet away from them
Alejandro was listening to the exchange. 'I'm sorry, I
can't,' she answered awkwardly.

'I'll keep on asking,' Jeremy warned her.

Jemima almost winced at that unnecessary assurance, as she had already discovered that Jeremy, the
local estate agent and a divorcee in his early thirties,
had the hide of a rhinoceros when it came to taking a
polite hint that a woman wasn't interested. Since the day
she had signed the rental agreement on her cottage, he
must have asked her out at least a dozen times.

Aware of the glacial cool of Alejandro's scrutiny,
Jemima hastened to slot her key into the lock on the
front door.

'Why didn't you just tell him that you were married?'

'He already knows that. Everybody knows that,'
Jemima fielded irritably, making a point of flexing the
finger that bore her wedding ring as she pushed open
the door. 'But he also knows that I'm separated from
my husband.'

'There's nothing official about our separation,'

Alejandro countered, crowding her with his presence in the tiny hall before he moved on into the small living room. 'But I am surprised that you're still wearing the ring.'

Jemima shrugged a slight shoulder and made no reply as she unbuttoned Alfie's jacket and hung it up beside her fleece.

'Juice.' Alfie tugged at her sleeve.

'Please,' Jemima reminded him.

'Peese,' Alfie said obediently.

'Do you want coffee?' Jemima asked Alejandro grudgingly. He had taken up a stance by the window and his height and wide shoulders were blocking out a good deal of the light.

'*Sí,*' Alejandro confirmed.

'Peese,' Alfie told him helpfully. 'Say peese.'

'*Gracias,*' Alejandro pronounced in his own tongue, stubborn to the last and barely sparing the attentive toddler a glance.

Once again Jemima was taken aback by that pronounced lack of interest in her child. She had expected Alejandro to be stunned by Alfie's existence and, at the very least, extremely curious. 'Haven't you got any questions to ask me about him?' she enquired, her attention resting pointedly on Alfie's dark curly head as he crouched down to take his beloved cars out of the toy box and line them up in a row.

Alfie liked things organised and tidy, everything in its place. She had a sudden disconcerting recollection of Alejandro's immaculately neat desktop at the castle and wondered if there were other similarities that she had simply refused to see.

'When the family lawyer engages a solicitor here

to represent my interests, they can ask the questions,' Alejandro responded very drily.

'So, you're already convinced he's not yours,' Jemima breathed in a very quiet tone, her lips sealing over her gritted teeth like a steel trap.

Luxuriant black lashes swept up on Alejandro's gorgeous dark golden eyes, his handsome mouth taking on a sardonic cast. 'How could he be?'

Seething frustration filled Jemima. For a crazy instant, she wanted to jump on him and kick him and punch him, batter him into a state where he would be forced to listen to her. But she wasn't a violent woman and if he didn't listen to her, or believe in her, or even trust her, and he never had, at this stage of their relationship he probably never would. Wasn't that another good reason as to why she had walked out on their marriage? The conviction that she was beating her stupid head up against a brick wall? Not to mention the sheer impossibility of staying married to a man who was utterly convinced that she had had an affair with his brother?

While she waited on the kettle in the galley kitchen, she reached a sudden decision and lifted the wall phone to call Flora, asking her friend if it would be possible for her to look after Alfie for an hour. 'Alejandro is here,' she explained stiffly.

'Give me five minutes—I'll come down and pick Alfie up,' Flora promised.

Jemima set a china mug of coffee down near Alejandro. She knew what she had to do next but she just didn't want to. Been there, done that, got the T-shirt and the scars. Flora arrived very quickly, bridging the awkward silence with her chatter while Jemima fed Alfie into his coat again.

'Alejandro…Flora,' Jemima performed the introduction stiffly.

'I've heard so much about you,' Flora said brightly to Jemima's husband. 'None of it good.'

Alejandro sent Jemima a censorious look of hauteur and she reddened, wishing that the other woman had kept quiet rather than revealing how much she knew about her friend's marital problems.

The silence left after Flora's departure spread like a sheet of black ice waiting to entrap the unwary. Jemima straightened her slight shoulders, her blue eyes so dark with strain they had the glimmer of purple against her skin. 'I hate that I have to say this again, but you don't give me much choice—I did *not* sleep with your brother.'

Alejandro shot her a grim dark-eyed appraisal. 'At least he had the courage not to deny the charge—'

'Oh…right,' Jemima sliced in, rage bubbling and pounding through her like a waterfall that had been dammed up inside her. 'Marco didn't deny it, so therefore I have to be lying!'

'My brother has never lied to me but you have,' Alejandro pointed out levelly.

Jemima's hands clenched into fists. 'What lies? What are you talking about?'

'You went through thousands and thousands of pounds while we were still living together, yet you had nothing to show for your extravagance and could not even cover your own expenses in spite of the generous allowance I gave you. Somewhere in that financial mess, when I asked you for an explanation, there must have been lies,' he concluded.

Jemima had turned white as milk, for those were

charges she could not deny. She *had* got through a terrifying amount of money, although she hadn't spent it on herself. Sadly, she had had nothing to show for it, however, and she had found herself in the embarrassing position of not being able to pay bills during the last weeks of their marriage. All her sins had come home to roost by then, all because of the one seemingly harmless and seemingly even sensible little lie that she had told him when they'd first met.

'Did you give all that money to Marco?' Alejandro asked her abruptly, his voice harsh. 'He often overspent and I was afraid that he might have approached you for a loan.'

For a split second, Jemima was tempted to tell another lie to cover herself and then shame pierced her and she bent her head, refusing to look at him. Although, while on one level she was still angry with Alejandro's brother for dropping her in the mire by refusing to deny the allegations of an affair, she still retained enough fondness for the younger man not to seek revenge and to tell the truth. 'No, Marco never once asked me for money.'

Alejandro's lean, powerful body had tautened. He flicked her a narrowed glance so sharp that she was vaguely surprised it didn't actually cut her. 'I assume that you are still in contact with my brother?'

That comment startled her. 'No, I'm not. I haven't talked to Marco since I left Spain.'

Alejandro made no attempt to hide his surprise at that news. 'I'm amazed, when you were so intimate.'

Her teeth clenched at that crack. Not for the first time she was tempted to give way and simply tell him the truth. Unfortunately the repercussions threatened to be too great. Furthermore she had once faithfully promised Marco that she would never betray him. After all, she had seen for herself and on more than one occasion why the younger man was quite so determined to keep that particular secret from his family. Unfortunately, Marco's selfishness did not release her from her pledge of silence. In any case, she reminded herself ruefully, it was not solely Marco's fault that her marriage to his brother had broken down.

'Marco has been working in New York at our art gallery for the past couple of years. You haven't had any contact with him at all?' Alejandro persisted in a silky smooth tone, his accent growling along the edges of every syllable.

'But presumably he is supporting his child?'

'Alfie is not his bloody child!' Jemima raked at him furiously.

'There is no need to swear,' Alejandro murmured smooth as glass.

Jemima trembled and struggled to master a temper that was threatening to overwhelm her. Two years ago when she walked out on her marriage she had been exhausted and worn down to the bone by the weight of her secrets, but since then she had made a strong recovery. 'Alfie is not Marco's son,' she pronounced flatly.

'Your child is only the smallest bone of contention between us,' Alejandro intoned in a driven undertone, his stunning eyes full of condemnation bright as sunlight in his lean, saturnine face.

'Is that so?' Jemima asked tightly, ridiculously annoyed that he could so easily dismiss Alfie's existence as an unimportant element.

Alejandro bit out an unamused laugh. 'You know

surprisingly little about men,' he breathed roughly. 'I'm much more interested in what you *did* in my bed with my brother and why you felt the need to do it.'

In one comprehensive sentence, he tore down the deceptive veil of civility and confronted her with the reality of his convictions and she was shocked into silence by that direct attack. The experience also reminded her that she had never found Alejandro's moods or actions easy to predict and had often failed to identify the whys and wherefores that drove that hot-blooded temperament of his.

'Did you *have* him in our bed?' Alejandro gritted, lean brown hands clenched so hard by his side that she could see the white of bone over his knuckles. Intimidated, she stepped away, which wasn't easy to do in that small room and her calves pressed back against the door of the pale modern cupboard unit behind her.

In the inflammable mood he was in she didn't want to engage in another round of vehement denials, which he had already heard and summarily dismissed two years earlier. 'Alejandro…' she murmured as quietly as she could, trying to ratchet down the tension in the explosive atmosphere.

He flung his dark head back, his brilliant gaze splintering over her so hard that she would not have been surprised to see a shower of sparks light up the air. For a timeless moment and without the smallest warning she was entrapped by his powerfully sexual charisma and it was like looking into the sun. She remembered the hum of arousal and anticipation that had once started on the rare nights he was home on time for dinner, when she knew he would join her in their bedroom and take her to a world of such joyous physical excitement that she would briefly forget her loneliness and unhappiness.

'Is my need to know such sordid details too raw for you? Did you ever once stop to think of what it might be like for me to be forced to picture my wife in my brother's arms?' Alejandro ground out wrathfully.

'No,' she admitted, and it was the truth because she had never been intimate with Marco in that way and had wasted little time wondering how Alejandro's offensive and unfounded suspicions might be making him feel. Angry with her? Disillusioned? She had already been much too familiar with the knowledge that he had to be experiencing such responses while she failed to live up to the steep challenge of behaving like a Spanish countess.

'No, why should you have?' Alejandro growled, his accent thick as treacle on that rhetorical question. 'Marco was simply a sacrifice to your vanity and boredom, a destructive, trashy way of hitting back at me and my family—'

'That's absolute nonsense!' Jemima flailed back at him furiously.

'Then why did you ever let him touch you? Do you think I haven't wondered how it was between you?' Alejandro slung back bitterly. 'Do you think it didn't hurt to imagine you naked with him? Sobbing with gratification as he pleasured you? Crying out as you came?'

'Stop it!' Jemima launched at him pleadingly, her face hot with mortification at the pungent sexual images he was summoning up. 'Stop talking like that right now!'

'Does it strike too closely for you?' Alejandro hissed

fiercely. 'You got off lightly for being a faithless, lying slut, so stop staring at me with those big shocked eyes. I won't fall for the little-fragile-girl act this time around— I *know* you for what you are.'

Disturbed by the implicit threat in those hard words, Jemima spun away and walked past him to the window, fighting to get a grip on the turmoil of her emotions. He had shocked her, he had shocked her very deeply, for it had not until that moment struck her that his belief in her infidelity could have inflicted that much damage. Two years back when he had confronted her about Marco, he had been cold, controlled, behaving almost as though he were indifferent to her. By then she had believed that Alejandro felt very little for her and might even be grateful for a good excuse to end their unhappy alliance. Only now did she recognise that she had been naïve to accept that surface show from a male as deep and emotional as he could be.

'I'm not a slut because I didn't have an affair with your brother,' Jemima muttered heavily, slowly turning back round to face him. 'And you should know now that my son, Alfie, is your son.'

'Is that supposed to be a joke?' Alejandro demanded with a look of angry bewilderment. 'I'm well aware that you suffered a miscarriage before you left Spain.'

'We *assumed* I had had a miscarriage,' Jemima corrected with curt emphasis. 'But when I finally went to see a doctor here in the UK, I discovered that I was still pregnant. He suggested that I might have initially been carrying twins and lost one of them, or that the bleeding I experienced was merely the threat of a miscarriage rather than an actual one. Whatever,' she continued doggedly, her slender hands clenching tightly in on themselves beneath his incredulous appraisal, 'I was still very much pregnant when I arrived in England and Alfie was born just five months later.'

Alejandro dealt her a seething appraisal, his disbelief palpable. 'That is not possible.'

Jemima yanked open a drawer in the sideboard and leafed through several documents to find Alfie's birth certificate. In one sense she could not credit what she was doing and yet in another she could not see how she could possibly do anything else. Her son was her husband's child and that was not something she could lie about or leave in doubt because she had to take into account how Alfie would feel about his parentage in the future. It was a question of telling the truth whether she liked it or not. Emerging with the certificate, she extended it to Alejandro.

'This has to be nonsense,' Alejandro asserted, snatching the piece of paper from her fingers with something less than his usual engrained good manners.

'Well, if you can find some other way of explaining how I managed to give birth to a living child by that date and it not be yours, I'd like to hear it,' Jemima challenged without hesitation.

Alejandro stared down at the certificate with fulminating force and then glanced up, golden eyes bright as blades and as dangerous. 'All this proves is that you must still have been pregnant when you walked out on our marriage. It does not automatically follow that the child is mine.'

Jemima shook her fair head and expelled her breath in a slow hiss. 'I know it doesn't suit you to hear this news now and I really didn't want to tell you. Too much water has gone under the bridge since we split up and now we lead separate lives. But the point is, I can't lie to you about it. Some day Alfie may want to look you up and get acquainted.'

Alejandro studied her with brooding dark ferocity. 'If what you have just told me is the truth, if that little boy does prove to be mine, it was vindictive and extremely selfish of you to leave me in ignorance!'

Jemima had paled. 'When I left you I had no idea that I was still pregnant,' she protested.

'Two years is a long period of time, yet you made no attempt to inform me that I might be a father,' he fielded harshly. 'I will want DNA tests to confirm your claim before I make any decision about what I want to do.'

Jemima compressed her lips hard at the reference to the testing. Once again Alejandro was insulting her with the assumption that she had been an unfaithful wife and that, for that reason, there could be doubt over who had fathered her child. 'Do as you like,' she told him curtly. '*I* know who Alfie's father is and there has never been any doubt of his identity.'

'I will make arrangements for the tests to be carried out and I will see you again when the result is available,' Alejandro drawled, with lashings of dark Spanish masculine reserve emanating from his forbidding demeanour and cool taut intonation.

'I'll contact a solicitor and start the divorce,' Jemima proffered in turn, determined not to leave him with the impression that he was the only one of them who could act and make decisions.

Alejandro frowned, dark eyes unlit by gold narrowing in a piercing scrutiny that made her uncomfortable. 'It would be foolish to do anything before we have that DNA result.'

'I disagree,' Jemima flashed back at him angrily. 'I should have applied for a divorce the minute I left you!'

Cool as ice water, Alejandro quirked an ebony brow. 'And why didn't you?'

Jemima dealt him a fulminating glance but said nothing, merely moving past him to yank open her front door in a blunt invitation for him to leave. She was shaken to register that she was trembling with temper. She had forgotten just how angry and frustrated Alejandro could make her feel with his arrogant need to take charge and do exactly what he wanted, regardless of other opinions.

'I'll be in touch,' he delivered on the doorstep.

'I'd appreciate some warning the next time.' Jemima lifted a business card off the table and gave it to him. 'Phone and tell me when you're coming.'

Anger shimmering through her, she slammed the door in his wake and peered out from behind the shelter of the curtains to watch him swing into his fancy car and drive off.

Nothing had changed, she reflected unhappily. Even being in the same room again as Alejandro revived all the doubts, insecurities and regrets she had left behind her when she gave up on being his wife...

CHAPTER THREE

JEMIMA left her teenaged babysitter in charge of the house and closed the front door as quietly as she could behind her. Thursday nights she and Flora went to choir practice and enjoyed a convivial evening in the company of friends. As a rule she looked forward to getting out. But, recently, Jemima had been in a thoroughly bad mood and indeed was still stiff with the angry resentment that she had been struggling to suppress for two long weeks.

'Cheer up,' Flora urged as the two women walked in the direction of the quaint little medieval stone church and village green that made Charlbury St Helens so pretty a village. 'You're letting this whole DNA-testing business eat you alive and it's not healthy for you.'

Jemima flung her friend an apologetic glance. 'I can't help feeling as though I've been publicly humiliated by it,' she confessed ruefully.

'Both the notary and the GP are bound by rules of confidentiality,' Flora reminded her with a reassuring glance. 'I seriously doubt that either will discuss your private business with anyone, particularly if it may end up in a civil courtroom.'

Unconvinced, but recognising her friend's generous

attempt to offer comfort, Jemima compressed her lips, not wanting to be a bore on the subject, even though the DNA tests had proved to be an exercise in mortification in which she felt that her anonymity and privacy had been destroyed. When such tests were required for a case that might end up in a court they had to be done in a legal and formal manner. A snooty London solicitor acting on Alejandro's behalf had phoned her to spell out the requirements. Jemima had had to make an affidavit witnessed by a public notary as well as have photos taken to prove her identity before she could have the tests for her and Alfie done by her own GP. The actual tests had been swabs taken from the mouth and completed in seconds, but Jemima had writhed in mortification over the simple fact that both the notary and the doctor were being made aware of the fact that her husband doubted that Alfie was his child. She knew that she would never, ever forgive Alejandro for forcing her to undergo that demeaning process, all because he was convinced that she had broken her marriage vows.

Yet how could she have refused the tests when refusal would have been viewed as a virtual admission of wrongdoing? she asked herself as she moved into the comparative warmth of the church and greeted familiar faces with a wave and a determined smile. Common sense told her that it was essential that Alfie's father should know the truth; for Alfie's sake there should be absolutely no doubt on that score in anyone's mind. Those were the only reasons why she had agreed to the tests being carried out.

The effort of raising her voice in several rousing choruses and then singing a verse solo in her clear sweet soprano took Jemima's mind off her combative feelings.

She was definitely feeling more relaxed by the time she helped to stack the chairs away. Fabian Burrows, one of the local doctors and a very attractive male in his mid-thirties, reached for her jacket before she did and extended it for her to put on.

'You have a really beautiful voice,' he told her.

'Thanks,' she said, her cheeks warming a little beneath his keen appraisal.

He fell into step beside her and Flora. 'Are you going for a drink?' he asked, a supportive hand settling to her spine as she stumbled on the way down the church steps.

'Yes.'

'Fancy trying The Red Lion for a change?' he suggested, coming to a halt by the church gate while other members of the choir crossed the road to the usual hostelry.

'Thanks, but I'm with Flora,' Jemima told him lightly.

'You're both very welcome to keep me company,' he imparted while Jemima tried frantically to interpret the frowning meaningful expression on her friend's face. Did that look mean that Flora wanted to take up the invitation or that she didn't?

'I'm afraid this isn't a good night,' Flora remarked awkwardly, turning pointedly to look out onto the road.

Jemima saw the sports car parked there a split second before she saw the tall dark male sheathed in a cashmere overcoat leaning up against the bonnet and apparently waiting for her. Dismay gripped her and then temper ripped through her tiny frame like a storm warning. After all, she had specifically asked Alejandro to give her notice of his next intended visit. How dared he just turn up again without giving her proper notice of his plans?

But somehow the instant her attention settled on

Alejandro an uninvited surge of heat shimmied over her entire skin surface and sexual awareness taunted her in tender places. His dangerous sensuality threatened her like the piercing tip of a knife. Scorching dark golden eyes set in a lean dark-angel face assailed her and suddenly it was very hard to breathe because, no matter how angry she was with him, Alejandro was still drop-dead gorgeous and sinfully sexy. Even the lean, well-balanced flow of his powerful body against his luxurious car was elegant, stylish and fluid with grace. She wanted to walk past him and act as if he were invisible while the compelling pull of his attraction angered her almost as much as his unexpected appearance.

'How did you know where I was?'

'The babysitter,' Alejandro told her softly. 'My apologies if I'm intruding on your evening.'

'Who is this?' Fabian demanded loftily.

'Oh, I'm just her husband,' Alejandro drawled in a long-suffering tone that made Jemima's teeth grind together in disbelief.

The other man stiffened in discomfiture and muttered something about seeing Jemima the following week at practice. Turning to address Flora, who was also hovering, Fabian escorted her away.

'How *dare* you say that and embarrass him?' Jemima hissed like a spitting cat at Alejandro.

Alejandro, very much in arrogant Conde Olivares mode, gazed broodingly down at his diminutive wife. 'It is the truth. Every time I come here you're knee-deep in drooling men and flirting like mad.'

'You don't have the right to tell me how to behave any more.' Jemima threw those angry words back at him in defiance of the manner in which he was looking down at her.

Alejandro closed lean, strong hands over her shoulders and, dark eyes glittering like polished jet in the moonlight, he hauled her close and his wide sensual mouth plunged down on hers in an explosion of passion that blew her defences to hell and back. She hadn't been prepared, hadn't even dreamt that he might touch her again, and she was so taken aback that she was totally vulnerable. Her legs wobbled below her as the fiery demand of his mouth sent a message that hurtled through her slight body like a shriek alarm and awakened the desire she had shut out and denied since Alfie's birth.

In an equally abrupt movement, Alejandro straightened, spun her round and pinned her between his hard muscular length and the car. A gasp of relief escaped her as he pressed against her for, at that moment, pressure was exactly what her body craved; indeed, in the grip of that craving she had no shame. Her breathing was as ragged as the crazy pulse pounding in her throat while he ground his hips into her pelvis and heat and moisture burned between her thighs.

'*Dios mio! Vamonos*…let's go,' Alejandro urged raggedly, pulling back from her to yank open the car door. He almost lifted her nerveless body into the leather passenger seat and with a sure hand he protected the crown of her head from a painful bump courtesy of the roof.

'Let's go,' he said. Let's go where? she almost shouted back in response. But she hid from that revealing question to which she already knew her own answer while being fully, painfully aware of what her body longed for. She shrank into the seat as he clasped the seat belt round her and then bent her buzzing head, her hands closing over her knees to prevent them from visibly shaking in his presence.

She had trained herself to forget what that desperate, yearning, wanting for him could feel like and she did not want to remember. But the taste of him was still on her lips, just as the phantom recall of his hands on her still felt current while the slow burn pain of his withdrawal of contact continued to shock-wave through her and leave her cold.

'We really shouldn't touch in public places,' Alejandro intoned soft and low.

Jemima clenched her teeth together, hating herself for not having pushed him away. How dared he just grab her like that? How dared he prove that he could still make her respond to him? Of course, had she known what he was about to do she would have rejected him as he deserved, yes, she definitely would have, she reasoned stormily. But back when she had still been living with him, she had *always* wanted him. Need had been like a clawing ache inside her whenever she looked at him and the only time she had felt secure was when she was in his arms and she could forget everything else. Hugging that daunting memory to her, she hauled a stony shell of composure round her disturbed emotions, determined not to let him see how much he had shaken her up.

'You still haven't told me what you're doing here,' Jemima complained as he followed her to her front door.

'We'll talk inside.'

Jemima had to swallow back a sharp-tongued comment. In every situation Alejandro assumed command and that he rarely got it wrong only annoyed her more. She went in to her babysitter and paid her. Audra lived only two doors down from her and the arrangement suited both of them.

'Do you make a habit of leaving a child in charge of a child?' Alejandro enquired.

'No, I don't,' Jemima countered curtly. 'And though Audra may look immature, she's eighteen years old and training to be a nurse.'

Alejandro did not apologise for his misapprehension. Jemima hung up her jacket and hovered, her face burning as she remembered the heat of that extravagant kiss.

'It's a little late for a social call,' she remarked flatly, avoiding any visual contact with him, refusing to knuckle down and play hostess.

'I wanted to see my son,' Alejandro confided in a roughened undertone.

The import of that admission engulfed her like a tidal wave. So the DNA testing had delivered its expected result and backed up her claims, and thanks to that he now had to accept that she had not been lying to him yet he had not opened the subject with the fervent apology that he owed her. Her chin came up at a truculent angle. 'Alfie's asleep.'

'I don't mind looking at him while he sleeps,' Alejandro confessed in a not quite steady rush, his excitement at even that prospect unconcealed.

For a split second that look on his face softened something inside her but she fought it. 'But you didn't believe me when I told you he was yours—'

'Let's not get into that. I know the truth now. I know he is my child. I only got the news this morning. This is the soonest I could get here.'

His eagerness to see Alfie dismayed her, even while

she tried to tell herself that his reaction was only to be expected. He had just found out that he was a father. Naturally he was much more interested in Alfie than he had been when he had assumed that her son was some other man's. 'I'll take you upstairs,' she offered, striving to take control of the situation.

Alejandro moved quietly into the bedroom in Jemima's wake and studied the sleeping child in the wooden cot. Black curls tousled, with his little sleep-flushed face, Alfie looked peaceful and utterly adorable to his besotted mother's eyes. Alejandro closed a strong hand over the cot rail and stared down, spiky black lashes screening his gaze from her.

Without warning Alejandro looked across the cot at her, brilliant dark eyes brandishing a fierce challenge. 'I want to take him home to Spain.'

That announcement hit her like a bucket of icy water, shocking her and filling her with fear for the future. She backed away to the door and watched Alejandro award his son an undeniably tender last glance. Yes, he could be tender when he wanted to be but it wasn't a notion that took him very often, she conceded painfully. He had looked at her the same way the day they learned that she had conceived and his initial unconcealed pleasure in the discovery that she was pregnant had made her swallow back and conceal her own very different feelings on the same score. Yet how could she recall those confusing reactions now when Alfie had since become the very centre of her world? Given the chance she would never have turned the clock back to emerge childless from her failed marriage, but it was already beginning to occur to her that a childfree marriage would have been easier to dissolve.

I want to take him home to Spain. That frank declaration raced back and forth inside her head as she led the way back downstairs. It was only natural that Alejandro would want to show Alfie off to his family while ensuring that Alfie learnt about the magnificent heritage and ancestry that he had been born into on his father's side, she reasoned, eager not to overreact to his announcement.

'What did you mean when you said you wanted to take him back to Spain?' Jemima heard herself ask abruptly.

Alejandro took off his heavy cashmere overcoat and draped it on a dining chair by the table that filled the small bay window in the living room. His elegant charcoal-grey business suit accentuated his height. His classic profile was cool and uninformative when he turned back to her but his stunning dark eyes were bright gold chips of challenge.

'I cannot allow you to have full custody of my son,' Alejandro spelt out without apology. 'I don't believe that you can offer him what he needs to thrive in this environment. I wish I could say otherwise. I have no desire to fight you for custody of our child but I do not see how I can do anything else without betraying my duty to him.'

'How...*dare*...you?' Jemima threw back at him in a fiery temper of disbelief, her heart racing as if she were running a marathon. 'I gave birth to your precious son alone and unsupported and I've been on my own ever since. Alfie is a very happy and well-adjusted little boy and you know nothing about him, yet the minute you find out he exists you assume that I am an unfit parent!'

'Does he even know he has a father or a family in Spain? Is he learning to speak Spanish? What kind of stability can you give him? You are not a responsible person.'

'What gives you the right to say that to me?' Jemima interrupted thinly, her hands clenching into defensive fists by her side.

His lean, darkly handsome face tautened into censorious lines. 'Look at the way you dealt with our marriage, your debts, your affair with my brother—'

'For the last time, I did not have an affair with your brother!'

'You don't deal with problems, you run away,' Alejandro condemned without hesitation. 'How could you possibly raise our child properly and teach him what he needs to know?'

'I don't have to stand here putting up with being criticised by you any more. We're separated,' Jemima rattled out, her voice brittle. 'I want you to leave.'

Alejandro grabbed up his coat. 'It's impossible to talk to you,' he vented in a driven undertone of frustration.

'You call threatening to take my child away from me *talking*?' Jemima exclaimed with incredulous force. 'How did you expect me to respond to a threat?'

'A threat is something that may not happen, but I will most assuredly fight you for custody of my son,' Alejandro extended grittily, refusing to back down.

Jemima breathed in deep and slow to calm her jangling emotions and studied him with angry, anxious eyes. 'What can I do or say to convince you that I am a good mother?'

Having donned his coat, Alejandro shrugged a broad shoulder as if she was asking him the unanswerable.

Jemima's thoughts were already ploughing ahead to reach several fear-inducing conclusions. If a custody battle went to court, Alejandro had the wealth to hire the very best lawyers and nobody representing her interests would be able to compete. The very fact that she had kept quiet about Alfie's existence for the first two years of his life would weigh against her. And how much importance might a judge lay on the truth that Alfie would one day be an influential member of the Spanish aristocracy in charge of a massive country estate and a very successful string of international family businesses? Such a background and his father's ability to prepare his son for those responsibilities could not be easily ignored.

'You can't do this to me,' Jemima protested. 'I love Alfie and he loves and needs me.'

'Perhaps it is my turn to be a parent for a change,' Alejandro said drily, tugging open the front door to facilitate his departure with an alacrity that was ironically no longer welcome to her. 'When it comes to sharing one little boy a divorce will leave few, if any, equitable solutions possible. We will both have to compromise.'

Jemima reached out in an ill-considered movement to thrust the door he had opened closed again before sliding between it and him like an eel. Violet eyes dark with strain in her pale heart-shaped face, she stared up at him and muttered tightly, 'We need to discuss this *now*!'

Alejandro sent her a sardonic glance. '*Madre mia*, you change direction with the wind. You told me to leave…'

Jemima gritted her teeth. 'Possibly I was a little hasty. I wasn't expecting you to already be making plans for Alfie. You annoyed me earlier. Why did you kiss me?'

Alejandro took a small step forward that trapped her between the wooden door and his lean, powerful body. 'Because I wanted to, *mi dulzura*.'

He called her 'sweetness' and she ran out of breath and rationality in the same instant. Awareness ran like a river of red-hot lava through her trembling length, her nipples swelling and blossoming like fire flowers while the tender flesh at the very heart of her burned and ached. The atmosphere was explosive and she couldn't fight the hunger stabbing at her. She studied the full curve of his sensual lower lip, reliving the taste of him, and slowly tipped her head back to meet hot golden eyes.

'Ask me to stay the night,' Alejandro urged thickly, pushing her back against the door, letting her feel the hard, promising power of his erection through his well-cut trousers. Air scissored through her lungs in a breathless surge, sexual heat uniting with dismay to hold her there.

'You want to stay?' Jemima whispered, already visualising closing a hand into the expensive fabric of his overcoat to haul him down to her, already imagining the taste and passion of him that drew her like a fire on a winter day. Desire had her in the fiercest of holds.

A long brown finger skimmed along the quivering line of her white throat, pausing to flick the tiny pulse flickering wildly above her collarbone. 'It's what you want too—'

'No,' Jemima gasped strickenly, feeling her self-discipline shatter like glass in the ambience and below it the roar of need she had resisted for so long.

'Liar,' Alejandro countered without hesitation, his confidence in his own powers of seduction absolute.

Her slender body vibrating with awareness, she still managed to tear free of him and step back. It hurt like hell. She couldn't think; she could only fight the craving that she recognised as a dangerous weakness. 'Leave,' she urged again, wanting to hug herself in consolation for the rush of cold and disappointment enveloping her.

'Call me when you come to your senses,' Alejandro drawled, hooded dark golden eyes undimmed by rejection as he tossed a business card down on the little shelf in the hallway.

And in a moment he was gone and she was left in a disturbing mess of conflicting emotions and regrets. She was furious with herself because she hadn't sorted out anything. Sex had got in the way and had only exacerbated the tensions between them. But she should have risen above the challenge to concentrate on Alfie and on Alejandro's threats. He had wanted to stay the night with her. He had wanted to share a bed with her again. The blood ran hot below her fair skin. For just a moment he had been as vulnerable as she to the powerful attraction that could still flare between them. She adjusted that thought the instant she thought it. No, Alejandro had *not* been vulnerable. If she had let him he would have slept with her again but it wouldn't have meant anything to him or led anywhere. He believed she had slept with Marco and he hated her for it. She lifted his business card and threw it down on the dining table in a fever of self-loathing. Alejandro was calling the shots again and she didn't like that at all.

Yet over three years earlier when they were dating

she had liked the way Alejandro had automatically taken charge and looked after her and had revelled in his masculine protective instincts. Looking back with hindsight, she marvelled at the way he had made her feel and how much maturity had changed her. Of course, she had been a virgin when they'd first met. As a result she had been far too quick to idealise Alejandro and believe that they had something special together. She had not even recognised him for the womaniser he was until one of the hotel maids had slid an old newspaper beneath her nose, pointed to a photo and said, 'Isn't that that Spanish guy you're seeing?'

And there Alejandro had been, pictured at some snobby London party with a beautiful blonde in an evening dress. The accompanying prose had made it clear that he enjoyed the reputation of a heartbreaker who always had more than one woman in tow. She hadn't wanted to believe the evidence even though Alejandro had already proved to be anything but a devoted boyfriend, cancelling dates as he did at the last minute and rarely phoning when he said he would. When she'd questioned him, however, Alejandro had been commendably frank.

'I'm not looking for a serious relationship,' he had told her without apology. 'I'm not interested in being tied down.'

Feeling stupid and hurt over the assumptions she had made and grateful that she had, at that stage, stayed out of his bed, Jemima had put the brakes on her feelings for him and had begun going out socialising again with her friends. Before very long she too was dating someone else, a local accountant who was flatteringly keen to offer her an exclusive relationship. But when Alejandro had realised that she was seeing another man, he had had a furious row with her, which had made it perfectly clear that, while he expected her to share him, he was not prepared to share her. For a few weeks they had split up and, although she was heartbroken at losing him at the time, she had thought it was the only option left.

Barely a month later, though, Alejandro had come back to her and had said that he would stop seeing other women. Jemima had been overjoyed and their relationship had entered a far more intense second phase. Head over heels in love with him as she had been, she had plunged straight into a passionate affair. He had rented a house not far from the hotel where she worked and they had spent every spare minute there together. In her entire life she had never known such happiness as she had known then, during the romantic weekends he'd shared with her. The demands of business and family, not to mention the fact that he lived in Spain, had often kept them apart when they wanted to be together, and on her twentieth birthday Alejandro had asked her to marry him. He had not said he loved her; he had *never* told her he loved her. He had merely said that he could not continue spending so much time in England with her. He had made marriage sound like a natural progression.

But he had not invited her to meet his family before they took that crucial final step. No doubt he had known how much his relatives would disapprove of his ordinary English bride, who had so little to offer on their terms. Within weeks of his proposal they had married in a London church with only a couple of witnesses present. She had had no idea at all of what his life in Spain would be like. In fact she had been a lamb to the slaughter in her ignorance.

Dragging herself free of wounding memories that still rankled, Jemima lifted her head high. That silly infatuated and insecure girl was dead and gone. This time around she was in control of her own destiny and, with that in mind, she snatched up her phone and rang Alejandro.

'We have to meet to talk about Alfie,' she told him urgently.

'Couldn't you have decided that while I was still with you?' Alejandro enquired drily.

'I'm not like you. I don't plan everything,' she reasoned defensively.

He suggested that she and Alfie meet him the following afternoon at his London apartment.

'I know you want to see Alfie again, but he would be better left out of it tomorrow—we'll probably argue.'

Having agreed a time and won his agreement on the score of Alfie, Jemima put down the phone again and wondered anxiously what rabbit she could possibly pull out of the hat that might persuade him that their son was better off living with his mother in England...

CHAPTER FOUR

THE London apartment was not the same one that Jemima remembered. The new one was bigger, more centrally located and sleek and contemporary in style, while the previous accommodation had been knee deep in opulent antiques and heavy drapes, a home-from-home backdrop for a family accustomed to life in a medieval castle.

A manservant showed her into a huge elegant reception room with the stark lines and striking impact of a modern artwork, again a very appropriate look for a family that owned a famous chain of art galleries.

She caught her reflection in the glass of an interior window and decided that, even though she was wearing the smartest outfit in her wardrobe, she looked juvenile in her knee-length black boots, short black skirt and red sweater. But her lifestyle no longer required dressy clothing and she preferred to plough her profits either back into the shop or into her savings. Having survived a childhood in which cash was often in very short supply, Jemima only felt truly safe now when she had a healthy balance in her rainy day account.

In the act of putting away a mobile phone, Alejandro emerged from an adjacent room to join her. His elegant black pinstripe suit and blue shirt fitted him with the expensive fidelity of the very best tailoring and the finest cloth, outlining broad shoulders, narrow masculine hips and long, long, powerful legs. Her attention locked to his lean dark features, noting the blue black shadow round his handsome jaw line, and for a split second she was lost in the memory of the rasp of stubble against her skin in the mornings. She could feel a guilty blush envelop her from her brow to her toes. His black hair still damp and spiky from the shower, Alejandro was the most absolutely beautiful man she had ever seen and her heart was jumping inside her as if the ground had suddenly fallen away beneath her feet.

'Is your friend looking after Alfie?' he enquired.

'Yes, but he attends a playgroup in the afternoons,' she explained.

She turned down an offer of refreshments and hovered while Alejandro helped himself to strong black coffee that scented the air with its unmistakeable aroma. Memories she didn't want were bombarding her again. He had taught her to grind coffee beans and make what he called 'proper' coffee. There had been so many things she didn't know about that he took for granted. He had even been a better cook than she was and right from the start she had been captivated by his knowledge and sophistication. But before their marriage—when things had gone wrong between them—he had scooped her up into his arms and swept her off to bed and she had been so ecstatic that she wouldn't have cared if the roof had fallen in afterwards. But once their sex life had ground to a halt, they'd had no means of communication at all and it had seemed natural to her that their marriage had then fallen apart. He had just lost interest in her, a development she had seen as being only a matter of time from the outset of their acquaintance.

'I couldn't sleep last night,' Jemima admitted in a sudden nervous rush, her eyes violet as pansies in the sunlit room. 'I was worrying about what you said about Alfie.'

'You named him Alfonso after my father. That was a pleasant surprise,' Alejandro remarked.

'He was named in memory of my grandfather, Alfred, as well,' Jemima advanced, not choosing to admit that the kindly vegetable-growing maternal grandfather she recalled had probably been the only presentable member of her former family circle, in that he had worked for a living and had stayed on the right side of the law. 'That's why I call him Alfie, because that was how my grandpa was known.'

Alejandro studied her with stunning dark golden eyes ringed and enhanced by black inky lashes. His charismatic appeal was so powerful that she couldn't take her attention off him and her mouth ran dry.

'We can't reasonably hope to share a child when we're living in different countries,' he told her.

Jemima tensed and smoothed her skirt down over her slight hips with moist palms. 'Other people manage it—'

'I want my son to grow up in Spain—'

'Well, you can't always have what you want,' Jemima pointed out flatly.

Alejandro set down his empty cup and strolled across the floor towards her. 'I too gave this matter serious thought last night. I can give you a choice...'

Her spine went rigid, her eyes flying wide with uncertainty. 'What sort of a choice?'

'Option one: you return to Spain and give our marriage another chance. Or, option two: I take you to court over Alfie and we fight for him.' As Jemima lost colour and a look of disbelief tautened her delicate pointed features Alejandro surveyed her with unblemished cool. 'From my point of view it's a very fair offer and more than you deserve.'

As an incendiary response leapt onto Jemima's tongue she swallowed it back and welded her lips closed, determined not to say anything before she had thought it through. But sheer shock was ricocheting through her in wave after wave. Alejandro was asking her to go back to him and live with him as his wife again? She was totally stunned by that proposition and had never dreamt that he would consider making it. 'That's a crazy idea,' she said weakly.

'If you take into account our son's needs, it's a very practical idea,' Alejandro contradicted levelly.

Jemima breathed in slowly and tried to concentrate her mind solely on her son's best interests, even though her brain was in a total fog at what he had just suggested. Many children might be more contented with two parents rather than one but that wasn't the end of the story. 'If we're not happy together, how could Alfie possibly be happy? I don't understand why you're even discussing the idea of us living together again.'

'Are you really that naïve?' His intent gaze was semi-screened by lush sooty lashes to a hot glitter of gold while the muscles in his strong jaw line clenched hard. 'I still want you. If I didn't I wouldn't be offering you this alternative.'

The heat of that look welded Jemima to where she stood and colour ran in scarlet ribbons into her cheeks.

Once again he had taken her by surprise. 'Are you saying that you're able to forgive me for the past?'

Alejandro loosed a harsh laugh of disagreement. 'No, I couldn't go that far. I'm saying that if I get you back into my bed, I will make the effort to overlook your past transgressions.'

Her bosom swelled with wounded pride and resentment as she drew in a very deep and steadying breath. 'Fortunately for me, I haven't the slightest desire to be married to you again. You may have considered it an honour the first time around, but for me it was more like living in purgatory.'

Alejandro dealt her a stony look that chilled her to freezing point and she knew that she had angered him. She recognised that he believed that he was making an enormously generous concession in offering her—an unfaithful wife—the opportunity to live with him again. She even recognised that lots of women would bite off his hand in their eagerness to accept such an offer. After all, he was drop-dead gorgeous, amazing in bed and open-handed with money…as long as you could tell him what you'd done with it, she completed inwardly and suppressed a shiver, flinching from her bad memories. But at heart Alejandro was as flint-hard and unyielding as his centuries-old castle. He believed she had betrayed him and he was not the forgiving type and would never come round to seeing or understanding her side of the story. He thought she was a slut and even if she lived with him for another twenty years he would die thinking that she was a slut.

'I've made a life for myself now in the village and I enjoy my life there,' Jemima responded in a stiff tone of restraint that did not come naturally to her. 'I was miserable in Spain and you didn't seem any happier with me as a wife. Why would you want to revisit the past?'

'Only because we have a son.' Alejandro gave her a sardonic appraisal. 'And this time around life could be much more straightforward.'

'How?' Jemima prompted baldly, wanting every detail of his thoughts even though she had no intention of accepting his offer.

'I know you for who you are now. I would have no false expectations, no sentimental ideas. Our marriage would merely be a convenient agreement for Alfie's benefit. All I would require from you would be the superficial show—'

'And sex,' Jemima added in a tight-mouthed undertone, because she felt demeaned that he had dared to include that aspect.

'Be grateful that you still have that much appeal, *mi dulzura*. Without the pull of that angle, I wouldn't even have considered taking you back.'

Clashing unwarily with hot golden eyes, Jemima experienced a deeply mortifying sliding sensation low in her pelvis. It infuriated her that she could still react to him that way when so much else was wrong between them. Her body took not the smallest account of her brain or even of common sense, for being attracted to Alejandro was destructive and stupid and likely to get her into serious trouble. It occurred to her that maybe he felt the same way about her and that was such a novel suspicion that she stared at him, wondering if he too could be fighting the same rearguard action against his own natural inclinations.

'You don't like the fact that you still find me attractive,' Jemima commented, daringly taking a stab in the dark.

'But I can handle it. Familiarity breeds contempt—isn't that what they say?' His brilliant eyes were lit by a sensual golden glimmer that as his gaze wandered over her seemed to burn over her skin like a tiny point of flame. 'I believe that this arrangement will give me a healthy chance of working you right out of my system.'

Jemima could not resist the sensual temptation of imagining what it would be like to be put to that kind of work in the marital bedroom. The more responsive parts of her treacherous body hummed with enthusiasm until shame and pride combined to suppress her facetious thoughts. She had never been able to escape the fear that wanting and loving any man as much as she had once loved and wanted Alejandro was weak and pathetic. It had inspired her into making numerous attempts to play it cool with him, most of which had blown up in her silly face as she had lacked both subtlety and good timing. She had acted all cool, for instance, once he'd stopped sleeping with her while she was pregnant; rather a case of closing the barn door after the horse had already bolted, she recalled impatiently. Those final weeks of their marriage he hadn't seemed to notice her at all and his increasing indifference and long working days had made her feel invisible and insignificant.

'I couldn't just go back to Spain,' she told him again. 'I've worked hard to build up my business. I don't want to lose it—'

'I'm willing to cover the cost of a manager for several months. That would give you the time and space to come up with a more permanent solution.'

Cut off at the knees by that unexpectedly practical proposal, Jemima muttered, 'I couldn't live with you again.'

'That decision is yours to make.' Alejandro shifted a broad shoulder in a fluid and fatalistic shrug, his lean, strong face full of brooding dark Spanish reserve and pride. 'But I've already missed out on two years of my son's life and I don't want to waste any more time. My English lawyer is waiting to hear whether or not I wish to proceed with a custody claim.'

That assurance hit Jemima like a bucket of snow thrown across unprotected skin. Every anxious cell in her body plunged into overload. 'Are you simply expecting me to make up my mind about this here and now?' she gasped.

Alejandro quirked an ebony brow. 'Why not? I'm not in the mood to be patient or understanding. I doubt that you suffered many sleepless nights while you were denying me the chance to get to know my son.'

In receipt of that shrewd comment on her attitude, Jemima turned almost as red as her sweater. It was true. She had pretty much celebrated her escape from Spain. She had regretted her failed marriage and cried herself to sleep many nights but she had blamed him entirely for that failure. Now sufficient time had passed for her to be willing to acknowledge that she, too, had made serious mistakes that had undoubtedly contributed to their break-up. She had certainly kept far too many secrets from him, had spent a lot of money, but that did not mean that she was prepared to have another go at their marriage. But she did, however, love her son very much and she did appreciate how much she had denied

Alejandro when she chose not to inform him that he was a father.

'I could come and stay in Spain for a few weeks,' she suggested limply as an alternative.

'A temporary fix of that nature would be pointless.'

'I couldn't possibly sign up to return to our marriage for the rest of my life. That's an appalling idea. Even convicts get time lopped off their sentences for good behaviour!' Jemima pointed out helplessly. 'Maybe I could consider coming out to Spain for a trial period, like, say…three months.'

Alejandro frowned. 'And what would that achieve?' he derided.

'Well, by then we would know if such an extraordinary arrangement was sustainable and I would still have a life to return to in the village if it wasn't working,' she argued vehemently. 'I'm not saying I will do it, but you would also have to give me a legal undertaking that you would not try to claim custody of Alfie while he was still in Spain because that would give you an unfair advantage.'

'The exact same advantage that you would have as an Englishwoman applying for custody in an English court,' Alejandro traded drily.

Her eyes fell before his at that response. 'But we just couldn't do it…*live* together again,' she protested in an enervated rush, folding her arms and walking round the room in a restive circle.

'There has never been a divorce in my family!'

'That's nothing to boast about. We're not living in the Dark Ages any more. People don't have to live with a mistake for ever.'

'But you think it's all right for our son to suffer all the disadvantages of coming from a broken home?'

Jemima groaned out loud in frustration, all shaken up at the very idea of reliving any part of their brief marriage. 'We can't make everything perfect for Alfie.'

'No, but it is our responsibility to give him the best of ourselves, even if that means making personal sacrifices. I respect that,' Alejandro intoned with insistent bite.

'You're always so superior. I want the best for Alfie too.'

'Yet you didn't see a problem bringing him up without a father,' Alejandro lashed back soft and low.

Her face flamed.

'If you truly do want the best for our son, come back to Spain.'

It was blackmail whichever way she looked at it: emotional blackmail, moral blackmail. He knew which buttons to push. He knew how to make her conscience writhe. He was too clever for her, she thought worriedly. If her best hadn't been good enough two years back, how much worse would she fare now with him? But had she ever really given him her best? a little voice asked her doggedly and the abstracted look in her gaze deepened. She was older and wiser and more confident, she reminded herself fiercely. Would it do her so much harm to give their marriage another shot? Of course it went without saying that it wouldn't work out and that both the trial and the subsequent break-up would hurt her again, but wouldn't agreeing give her the satisfaction of knowing that she had tried every option and made the best effort she could?

In the heat of that last inspiring thought, Jemima

turned back to focus on her tall, darkly handsome husband. 'All right. I'll come back to Spain but initially I'm only agreeing to stay for three months,' she extended, nervous tension rippling through her in a quivering wave as she realised what she was giving her consent to.

Alejandro stared back at her with brooding dark eyes, revealing neither satisfaction nor surprise at her surrender. 'I will accept that.'

Jemima gazed back at him, suddenly horrified at what she had allowed herself to be persuaded into. He had the silver tongue of the devil, she decided wildly. He had made her feel that any decent mother would have another go at being married for her child's sake. He had studied her with those smouldering dark golden eyes and told her that he *still* wanted her. Not only had she liked that news very much but her body had burned and her brain had shrivelled while she'd thought that truth through to its natural conclusion.

'Have you had lunch?' Alejandro asked.

Jemima backed away a step like a drug addict being offered a banned substance. 'No, but I'm not hungry. I think I should get back to the shop.'

'Of course, you'll have a lot of arrangements to put in place. I'll instruct a recruitment agency to find you a manager,' Alejandro imparted smooth as ice, gleaming dark golden eyes raking over her with a subdued heat that she felt as deep as the marrow of her bones. 'I don't want this to take too long. I also want to see Alfie.'

'Will you still be here over the weekend?' At his nod of assent, Jemima added breathlessly, 'Then come down and see him tomorrow.'

'How soon will you come to Spain?' he prompted.

'Just as soon as I can get it organised.'

'I should take you home,' Alejandro murmured before she got as far as the hall.

'No. I'm used to getting the train…'

'I'll take you to the station, *mi dulzura.*'

The immediate change in his attitude to her made a big impression on Jemima. All of a sudden he believed it was his job to look after her again and it felt seriously strange to have someone expressing concern on her behalf. She accompanied him down to the basement car park and climbed into his shiny car. As she clasped the seat belt Alejandro reached for her, a lean hand tugging up her chin so that his beautiful mouth could crash down on hers without anything getting in the way. It was like plugging her fingers into an electric socket or walking out unprepared into a hurricane. As he plundered her readily parted lips her hand rose and her fingers speared into his luxuriant black hair, holding him to her. The passionate pressure of his mouth on hers was a glorious invitation to feel things she hadn't felt in too long and the plunge of his tongue stoked a hunger she had never managed to forget.

'Dios mio! Te deseo.' He told her he wanted her in a voice hoarse with desire and it sparked a flame at the heart of her and made her shiver with shock. That fast, he had contrived to turn the clock back.

As Jemima drew back from him, breathless with longing and self-loathing, his brilliant gaze scanned her flushed face. 'If you stayed, I would give you so much pleasure.'

Jemima tore her stricken eyes from his, shame sitting inside her like a heavy rock because she was tempted. 'I'll see you on Saturday,' she said tightly.

All the way home on the train she was picturing his lean, strong features inside her head and tearing herself apart over what she had agreed to do. He might as well have hypnotised her! Sandy picked her up in the shop van and dropped her at Flora's cottage.

Twenty minutes later, Jemima was sitting at the island in her friend's kitchen with Alfie cradled half asleep on her lap from his afternoon exertions. Flora was studying her with wide and incredulous green eyes. 'Tell me you're not serious…I thought you hated your ex.'

Jemima shifted her hands in an effort to explain a decision that felt almost inexplicable even to her. 'What Alejandro said about giving our marriage another go for Alfie's sake made sense to me,' she confided ruefully. 'When I walked out on him I didn't know I was still pregnant and I'm not sure I would've gone if I'd known.'

Her friend's face was troubled. 'You were a bag of nerves when I first met you and you had no self-esteem. It's not my place to criticise your husband but if that's what being married to him did to you, something was badly wrong.'

'Several things were badly wrong then, but not everything was his fault.' Alfie snuggled into his mother's shoulder with a little snuffle of contentment and she rearranged his solid little body for greater comfort. 'Marco's living in New York now and another…er… problem I had, well, it's gone too,' she continued, her expressive eyes veiled as she thought back reluctantly to those last stressful months in Spain, which had been, without a doubt, the most distressing and nerve-racking period of her life.

'You want to give your marriage another chance,'

Flora registered in a tone of quiet comprehension. 'If that's what you really do want, I hope it works out the way you hope. But if it doesn't, I'll still be here to offer support...'

CHAPTER FIVE

FROM her stance on the edge of the small adventure playground, Jemima watched Alejandro park his sumptuous vehicle. Halston Manor estate lay a few miles outside the village and its grounds were open to the public the year round and much used by locals. Jemima had arranged their meeting with care, choosing an outdoor location where Alfie could let off steam and where all interaction between his parents would have to be circumspect.

Alejandro was dressed with unusual informality in a heavy dark jacket, sweater and jeans. Black hair ruffled by the breeze and blowing back from his classic bronzed features, he looked totally amazing and every woman in the vicinity awarded his tall ,well-built figure a lingering look. Jemima tried very hard not to stare and, shivering a little in the cool spring air, she dug her hands into the pockets of her red coat and focused on Alfie, who was climbing the steps to the slide, his big dark eyes sparkling with enjoyment.

'The family resemblance is obvious,' Alejandro remarked with husky satisfaction. 'He is very much a Vasquez, though he has your curls and there is a look of you about his eyes and mouth.'

'I've told him about you,' Jemima informed him.

'How did he take it?'

'He's quite excited about the idea of having a father,' she confided. 'But he doesn't really understand what a father is or what one does.'

In receipt of that news, Alejandro gave both Jemima and Alfie an immediate demonstration, striding forward to intervene when a bigger boy pushed his way past Alfie on the slide steps and the toddler nearly fell. Jemima watched as Alejandro grabbed her son and steadied him. Alfie laughed and smiled up at Alejandro, who spoke to him before stepping back to applaud Alfie's energetic descent of the slide.

Her attention glued to man and child, Jemima hovered. Father and son did look almost ludicrously alike from their black hair and olive-tinted skin to their dark eyes and the brilliance of their smiles. Alfie shouted at her to join them at the swings and she went over, her small face taut, her eyes wary. She could barely speak to Alejandro, yet they'd had a child together: it was an unsettling thought. She pushed Alfie on the swing and watched him show off for his father's benefit. Then her son jumped off the swing before it came to a halt and fell, bursting into tears of over-excitement.

Alejandro scooped him up and took him straight over to another piece of equipment to distract him and Alfie quickly stopped crying. Jemima hadn't expected Alejandro to be as assured at handling a young child as he so obviously was. She watched him crouch down to wipe Alfie's tear-wet face, and tensed as Alfie suddenly flung his arms round Alejandro and hugged him with the easy affection that was so much a part of him. She saw Alejandro's expression as well: the sudden blossoming warmth in his dark eyes, the tightening of his fabulous bone structure that suggested that he was struggling to hold back his emotions and the manner in which he vaulted upright to unashamedly hug Alfie back.

Set down again and in high spirits, Alfie scampered over to his mother and grabbed her hand. 'Ducks... ducks,' he urged and, turning his head, he called, *'Papa...Papa!'* in Spanish as if he had been calling Alejandro that all his life.

'Now we go and feed the ducks,' Jemima explained to Alejandro.

Alfie tearing ahead of them, they walked along the wide path by the lake.

'He's a wonderful little boy,' Alejandro commented abruptly, his dark, deep accented drawl low pitched and husky. 'You've done well with him.'

Jemima shot him a surprised glance and met gleaming dark golden eyes with an inner quiver. 'Thanks.'

'Only a happy, confident child could accept a stranger so easily.'

Warmed by that approval, Jemima felt less defensive and she leant back against a tree and relaxed while Alfie fed the ducks and talked to Alejandro about them. A lot of what the little boy said was nonsense-talk because he only had a small vocabulary, but Alejandro played along. Alfie stretched out a trusting hand to hold his father's and Alejandro began to tell his son about the lake at the Castillo del Halcón and the ducks that lived there.

'The recruitment agency got in touch yesterday and have promised to send me a couple of CVs by midweek,' she told him.

'Estupendo! Marvellous,' Alejandro pronounced,

studying her from below the dense black fringe of his lashes, eyes a glinting gold provocation that sent colour winging into her cheeks.

He looked at her and she could barely catch her breath. Her nipples were taut, distended buds beneath her clothing and her thighs pressed together as though to contain the rise of the hot, sensitised heat there. She swallowed hard, struggling to shut out the fierce sexual awareness that was racing through her veins like an adrenalin rush.

'Tell me,' Alejandro murmured in a lazy undertone as he towered over her, one lean brown hand braced against the tree, and there was absolutely no forewarning of what he was about to say. 'What did you get from Marco that you couldn't get from me?'

Jemima recoiled from him as though he had stuck a knife in hcr and moved away several steps, her face flushing, her eyes evasive and full of discomfiture.

'Naturally I want to know,' Alejandro added curtly. *So beautiful and so treacherous*, he reflected darkly. It was a fact he could not afford to forget.

Jemima threw her head up, her eyes purple with strong emotion. 'He talked to me, he took me places, he introduced me to his friends… He wanted my opinions and my company, which is more than you ever did!'

In receipt of that recitation of his brother's deceptive talents, Alejandro dealt her a forbidding appraisal. 'Primarily, Marco used you to get at me. He's a player and you found that out for yourself, didn't you? Did you or did you not tell me that you hadn't heard from my brother since you left Spain?'

At that retaliatory crack, furious mortification gripped Jemima for, of course, he was correct in that assumption. Put under pressure, Marco's friendship had lacked strength, permanence and true affection. Refusing to respond in kind, however, she set her teeth together and for what remained of Alejandro's visit she spoke mainly to Alfie and only when forced to his father.

A month later, a four-wheel-drive driven by an estate worker collected Jemima and Alfie from their flight to Spain. Jemima had hoped that Alejandro might pick them up personally but she was not surprised when he failed to appear. As she had learned when they were first married, Alejandro was always very much in demand and, as his wife, she was usually at the foot of his priorities list.

It was a recollection that could only annoy Jemima on the day that she had had to leave behind both the home and the business that she cherished. An excellent manager had taken over the shop. Jemima had put most of her possessions in storage so that the older woman could also rent her house. But all the work she had put into training as a florist, growing her client base for the shop and decorating her home now seemed pointless. On the other hand, she *had* only agreed to a three-month sojourn in Spain, Jemima reminded herself bracingly. Surrendering to Alejandro's blackmail had cost her dear but retaining custody of the little boy securely strapped in the car seat beside her was much, *much* more important to her.

The Castle of the Hawk sat on rocky heights above a lush wooded valley in the remote Las Alpujarras mountains, the last outpost of the Moors in Spain. Little villages with white flat-roofed houses and steep roads adorned the mountainsides while olive, orange and almond groves, grapevines and crops grown for biofuels flourished in the fertile soil. The Vasquez family had ruled their hidden valley like feudal lords for centuries and anyone seeing Alejandro, the current Conde Olivares, being greeted by deferential locals soon appreciated just how much weight that heritage still carried.

Agriculture alone, however, had proved insufficient to keep Alejandro's family in the style to which they had long been accustomed. His father had opened an art gallery in Madrid, but it had taken Alejandro—an astute businessman with the guts to take risks and an infinitely more ruthless edge—to turn that initial purchase into a hugely profitable and influential chain of international galleries. A hotel group and several financial enterprises had also been acquired by Alejandro and between the demands of his business empire and the running of the family estate Alejandro had very little time to spare.

He had always tried to maintain a low profile with the media at home and abroad. However, not only was he very photogenic and the bearer of an ancient title, but he had also, prior to his marriage, enjoyed a love life that was very newsworthy. Those facts, allied with his growing visibility in the business world, had ensured that he could no longer pass undetected and both their wedding and their break-up had, to Alejandro's intense annoyance, attracted newspaper coverage. For that reason, Jemima felt she should have been better prepared when she'd found cameras waiting at the airport earlier that day to record their departure for Spain, but she had been out of the limelight for so long that the appearance of the paparazzi had taken her completely by surprise.

Jemima would also have liked to have known how on earth word of her apparent reconciliation with her Spanish Count and the fact that they now had a child had reached the public domain. She did have very good reason to dread renewed media exposure. Indeed, just thinking about how those photos might cause trouble for her again made Jemima feel sick with apprehension. She was praying that the bad luck that had overtaken her some years earlier and trapped her between a rock and a hard place would not reappear to cause her and those connected with her even more damage and distress.

Endeavouring to bury her worries and control her nerves, Jemima drank in the beauty of the picturesque landscape while the heavy vehicle climbed a familiar road girded by a forest of oaks and chestnuts. The car finally pulled into a courtyard ringed by ornamental trees in giant pots that bore the family coat of arms. Alfie stared out with rounded eyes at the towering thirteenth century stone fortress that now surrounded them on three sides. Her youthful figure slender in casual jeans and a tangerine T-shirt, Jemima left Alfie in the car and rattled the knocker on the giant studded front door.

The door was opened by the middle-aged housekeeper, Maria, but she stepped back to give precedence to a stout older woman with greying hair who carried herself with a ramrod straight spine, her hard black eyes glinting with outrage.

'How dare you come back to my home?' Doña Hortencia erupted, barring the doorway.

Her daughter, Beatriz, hurried into view and twisted her hands together in an ineffectual protest. 'Jemima, how lovely to see you again... *Mamá*, please, *please*... we must respect Alejandro's wishes.'

Her sister-in-law's anxious, embarrassed face was painful to behold. That her loyalties were tearing her in two was obvious.

The driver carted over two suitcases while Beatriz stared out at the child she could see peering through the window of the estate vehicle. 'Oh, is that Alfie, Jemima? May I go and see him?'

For once impervious to her mother's mood, Beatriz hurried out to the car. The driver hefted up the luggage and stepped past Doña Hortencia with a subservient dip of his head.

'Good afternoon, Doña Hortencia,' Jemima said stoically, following the driver indoors with her flight bag on her shoulder. She was determined not to react in any way to the dirty looks she was receiving and believed that she was a good deal less likely to be bullied than she had been two years earlier. The older woman would certainly make the attempt but Jemima had learned to care less about the impression she made.

Aglow with satisfaction, Beatriz returned holding Alfie's little hand in hers. '*Mamá*, look at him,' she urged with enthusiasm.

Doña Hortencia gazed down at her first grandchild and her forbidding stare softened for an instant before she shot a grim glance at her daughter-in-law. 'This little boy, Alejandro's son and heir, is the one and only thing you have got right.'

Swallowing back the urge to retaliate in kind, Jemima said nothing. What was there to say? Alejandro's mother would never like her or accept her as an equal. Her son had married an ordinary working woman and a foreigner, rather than the wealthy Spanish aristocrat whom the older woman had thought his due, and Doña Hortencia was too stubborn, arrogant and prejudiced to revise her attitude. When Jemima had first come to the castillo, the Spanish woman had done everything possible to ensure that her daughter-in-law's daily life was as miserable as she could make it. This time around, however, Jemima had no plans to accept victimhood.

Beatriz accompanied Jemima up the carved staircase and made small talk as if her life depended on it. Dark gloomy oil portraits of Alejandro's ancestors lined the hall and landing walls. Serious though Alejandro so often was, Jemima reflected helplessly, he was a positive barrel of laughs when she compared him to his predecessors.

'Alejandro has engaged a nanny to help you with Alfie,' Beatriz announced.

'How very thoughtful of your brother,' Jemima remarked after a noticeable pause.

'Placida is the daughter of one of our tenants and a very able girl,' her companion extended anxiously.

Jemima did not want to make Beatriz feel uncomfortable. 'I'm sure she's perfect for the job.'

'This is the room I chose for Alfie,' Beatriz announced with pride, throwing wide the door on a fully furnished nursery complete with a cot, a junior bed and piles of toys. 'Of course, you may prefer to choose another.'

'This is lovely. Did you organise all the toys?'

Beatriz laughed. 'No, that was my brother. Can you believe that Alejandro went shopping for his son?'

'I wouldn't have believed it if you hadn't told me,' Jemima admitted, as Alejandro's dislike of shopping

was well known. Bitter as she was about finding herself
back in Spain, she could only be touched by the effort
he had made on Alfie's behalf. Equally quickly, however, her thoughts travelled in the opposite direction.
Of course, wouldn't Alejandro's actual presence mean
more than the purchase of expensive toys? In fact wasn't
Alfie receiving his first dose of the same benign neglect
that Jemima had once endured as Alejandro's wife?

Undisturbed by such deep and troubled mental rumi-
nations, Alfie pelted across the room to grab a toy car
with an eager hand. His aunt watched him, entranced.
'You must be so proud,' Beatriz remarked.

Not for the first time, Jemima felt sorry for Beatriz,
who was only thirty-five years old but very much on the
shelf of her mother's making, for no young man capable
of winning Doña Hortencia's approval had ever come
along. A dutiful daughter to the last, Alejandro's older
sister lived the sedate life of a much older woman.

Placida, the small dark-haired nanny, came to be introduced. After chatting for a while, Jemima left Alfie
with Placida and Beatriz and crossed the corridor. The
elaborate suite of tower rooms in which she had lived
with Alejandro before her pregnancy had brought all
sharing to an end was unrecognisable to Jemima at first
glance. All the furniture had been changed and a pale
yellow colour scheme had banished the dark ornate wall-
paper that she had once hated, but that Doña Hortencia
had informed her was hand-painted, exceedingly rare
and there for eternity. A maid was already busily un-
packing her cases and putting her clothes away in the
dressing room.

A weird and worrying sense of déjà vu was now
settling over Jemima. Alejandro's non-appearance at

the airport had first ignited the suspicion that she was about to discover that nothing had changed in the marriage she had left behind. He had also just demonstrated his engrained habit of taking authoritarian charge of anything and everything that came within his radius. In hiring Placida over her head, Alejandro had shown that only his opinion mattered and Jemima did not appreciate being made to feel superfluous in her child's life.

Once the maid had gone, Jemima went for a shower and padded through to the dressing room to extract fresh clothes. It was a shock to open the closets and find that they were already stuffed full of brand-new garments and the drawers packed with equally new lingerie, all of it in her size. Her own small collection of clothes looked shabby in comparison. Evidently, Alejandro, the guy who hated to shop even for himself, had ordered her a new wardrobe. Such generosity was very much his trademark but it made Jemima feel uncomfortable. Perhaps he didn't trust her to dress smartly enough. Perhaps her lack of formal fashion sense had once embarrassed him. Maybe that was why he had gone shopping for her...

Yet the prospect of dining with her haughty mother-in-law garbed like a poor relation in more humble clothing had surprisingly little appeal and Jemima succumbed to the temptation of the new clothes. She selected an elegant sapphire blue dress and slid her feet into delicate sandals before hurriedly going to check on Alfie. He was playing happily in the bath while Placida watched over him. Using her slightly rusty Spanish, Jemima established that Alfie had already eaten his evening meal and she returned to the bedroom.

While she was combing her rebellious hair into a less tumbled style the door opened and she froze. Alejandro, already in the act of removing his tie, appeared. His immaculate grooming was, for once, absent. Indeed, in the bright light of the sunset flooding into the room through the windows, his tailored suit looked crumpled and almost dusty, his black hair tousled, while a dark shadow of stubble heavily accentuated his angular jaw line. But, even with all those flaws taken into consideration, he *still* looked spectacular, awesomely masculine and awesomely sexy. As she studied him, her body reacting with treacherous enthusiasm even as her pride rejected those earthy responses, hot, heady anger threatened to consume her.

'I told Maria we would dine alone next door tonight. Give me ten minutes for a shower,' Alejandro urged her carelessly, but the scorching golden eyes that raked over the mane of strawberry-blonde curls framing her heart-shaped face, before roaming down to the pouting curves defined by the fine fabric of her dress, were in no way casual. That appraisal was so hot she was vaguely surprised that her body didn't start smoking and if anything that bold, sensually appreciative appraisal only increased her resentment.

'Where do you get the nerve to look at me like that?' Jemima launched at him in furious condemnation of that familiarity and the evident plan for a romantic meal for two. It would take a great deal more than that one tiny effort to turn her into the compliant wife he so obviously wanted and expected.

His well-shaped ebony brows drew together as he shed his jacket and embarked on the buttons of his shirt. 'You're too eye-catching to ignore,' he told her teasingly

Jemima was fighting to hang onto her temper. She

didn't need a crystal ball to tell her that it was never cool to rail at a man for keeping his distance and even less cool to complain of a lack of attention. So she spun away and glowered at her own frustrated reflection in a tall cheval mirror. Why should she give him the satisfaction of knowing that she had been disappointed when he failed to show up at the airport? Or when he didn't even take the trouble to phone to make a polite excuse for his absence from home? Yet that lack of consideration for her feelings was so familiar from the past that she couldn't help wanting to scream and shout in complaint.

'I'm such an idiot!' she suddenly exclaimed, unable to hold back her seething emotions and keep her tongue glued to the roof of her mouth any longer. 'Somehow I thought it would be different…that you'd make more of an effort to make this work this time—'

'What are you talking about?' Alejandro demanded in the act of shedding the shirt to reveal a superb bronzed muscular chest sprinkled with dark curling hair and a hard, flat stomach that easily met the attributes of the proverbial six-pack.

Jemima spun back to face him. A pulse was beating so fast at the foot of her throat that it was a challenge to find her voice. With every fibre in her body she was blocking out and refusing to respond to his mesmeric physical appeal. 'I arrived here a couple of hours ago. What did you think it would be like for me to be confronted with your mother before I even saw you again? Obviously it didn't occur to you that for once in your life you should have been here for me!'

'I left a message with my mother for you. Are you

saying that you didn't receive it?' Alejandro prompted in a tone of hauteur that only set her teeth on edge more.

'Your mother hates me like poison. Are you still so naïve that you think she would take the trouble to pass on a message to me?' Jemima fired back at him.

'If you didn't get the message, I can only apologise for the oversight,' Alejandro drawled smooth as glass, casting off the remainder of his clothes with incredible cool and strolling into the bathroom as lithe and strikingly naked as a sleek bronzed god.

That non-committal and reserved response made Jemima so mad, she was vaguely surprised that the top of her head didn't blow off. 'Don't pull that aristocratic indifference act on me to try and embarrass me into silence!' she hissed, stalking after him into the bathroom.

'Since when has it been possible to embarrass you into silence?' And with that cutting comeback Alejandro switched on the shower and forced her to swallow back her ire as she assumed that he could no longer hear her above the noise of the water beating down on the tiles.

But Jemima was so irate she still couldn't shut up. The suave assurance with which Alejandro had stripped off in front of her and calmly entered the shower had acted like an electric shock on an already raw temper. 'I hate you when you treat me like this!' she yelled.

While Alejandro showered, Jemima paced in the doorway, all recollection of her past unhappiness as his wife returning then and there to haunt her. Not for anyone would she go through that experience again! And yet hadn't she just signed up again for a rerun on Alfie's behalf? How could it benefit Alfie that she wanted to kill his father in cold blood?

The water switched off and the fleecy white towel on the tiled wall was snatched off the rail. Jemima was trembling and she wrapped her arms round herself. Alejandro reappeared with the towel knotted round his narrow hips, his damp black hair slicked back from his brow and his big powerful body still beaded with drops of moisture. He surveyed her with infuriating, deeply offensive assurance.

'You don't hate me. Of course you don't,' he told her drily.

'And how do you make that out? By the time that I walked out on our marriage, I couldn't *stand* you!'

Alejandro moved towards her and she backed into the bedroom. 'But why?' he queried in the most reasonable of voices. 'Because I had realised what you were up to with Marco? Because I asked you to explain what happened to all that money? Any man would have demanded answers from you.'

'First and foremost I left you because you wouldn't believe a word I said, but I *did* have lots of other good reasons,' Jemima flung, her eyes bright as violet stars below her fine brows as she challenged him.

Alejandro frowned darkly. 'I'm hungry. I want to get dressed and eat. I don't want to get into a big scene right now.'

Such a surge of rage shot through Jemima's tiny frame that she genuinely felt as though she had grown physically taller. 'Alejandro…there's never a right time with you. But I suggest that for once you look at what you did to contribute to the breakdown of our marriage and stop blaming me for everything that went wrong—'

'Leave the past behind us.'

'Don't you dare say that to me when you continually throw everything I did back at me!' Jemima hissed.

Alejandro groaned out loud. 'So, say what you have to say in as few words as you can manage.'

'You forced me to live under the same roof as your mother—'

'The castle is very large. Such living arrangements are common in Spain—'

'It was never that simple. Doña Hortencia loathes me and she made my life a misery the last time I was here. What did you ever do to stop her?' she condemned fiercely.

'You always exaggerate. How was your life made a misery?' Alejandro countered in a discouraging tone of disbelief.

'If I asked any of the staff to do anything they had to run it by your mother first because she insisted that she was still the mistress of this household. Usually, whatever I wanted I didn't get and I found that humiliating. She criticised everything I did, refused to speak to me at mealtimes when you weren't there and insulted me to my face in front of visitors. Ask your sister. Beatriz avoids trouble like the plague but she won't tell you any lies if you ask the right questions.'

Alejandro had screened his brilliant gaze and his wide sensual mouth was compressed by the time she had finished speaking. 'I'll check it out.'

Jemima knotted her hands into fists. 'So, you can't take my word on that either?'

'Since it looks as though I am destined to go hungry tonight, what else do I stand accused of?' Alejandro enquired with sardonic bite.

His derisive intonation made Jemima's teeth grind

together. She was shivering with temper and her gaze locked accusingly to his. 'It's your fault that I fell pregnant with Alfie!'

Alejandro studied her in obvious bewilderment. 'You love our son. You can scarcely hold his conception against me.'

'I did when I first discovered that I was pregnant. You chose to be careless with contraception but I paid the price for it,' she challenged, flushing as she recalled the passionate bout of lovemaking in the shower that had led to her unplanned pregnancy. 'We had only been married a few months and I was still quite young for motherhood. I didn't feel ready for a baby and being so sick while I was carrying him didn't help. It made me feel more trapped than ever here but you didn't understand how I felt, did you?'

'No, I didn't, but then you didn't tell me at the time,' Alejandro countered levelly. 'Naturally I realised that you were unhappy but I assumed that was because you were unwell. I would've thought that by now you would have put any bitterness behind you on that score.'

Jemima regarded him with seething resentment. 'So *you* get a clean slate while *I* get reminded of my every mistake?'

'Alfie is *not* a mistake, Jemima. He is most probably the best thing that ever happened to either of us,' Alejandro proclaimed in an undertone of driven emotion that was rare for him, his stunning golden eyes unusually eloquent.

Her eyes suddenly stung with prickling tears. 'I didn't mean that *he* was a mistake…'

'Then what *did* you mean?'

'You see, there you go again…thinking the very worst

of me!' Jemima launched accusingly, the swimming moisture in her eyes overflowing.

'No, I don't.' Alejandro reached for her slim shoulders in a sudden movement that took her by surprise and he pulled her up against his lean, powerful body. 'But it's hard for me to understand how you can love Alfie but still regret his conception.'

Jemima quivered with awareness as the heat of him penetrated her dress. 'I don't regret it any more.'

'Yet you're still blaming me for a moment's forgetfulness when you could equally well blame yourself.' His stunning dark golden eyes flamed over her upturned face.

As she met his gaze head-on a kind of crazy lethargy gripped Jemima. She could feel the slow pound of her blood through her veins, the racing beat of her heart in her ears and in the pit of her stomach the pull of that electrifying, shockingly strong craving that only he could ignite. He lowered his head and kissed her with unashamed hunger, his lips demanding, his tongue probing with ravishing skill, his teeth nipping at the soft underside of her generous lower lip in a way that made her release a long, shuddering moan of helpless response.

He kissed her until her heart hammered, until she was breathless and hot and no longer thinking straight. She *felt* the zip of her dress going down. She felt the garment shimmy down her arms and simply slide to her feet. As he lifted her up she kicked off her shoes and let him bring her down on the bed. She loved his strength, his unhesitating self-assurance. She knew that she couldn't pretend that she was being seduced against her will. She knew she wouldn't be able to tell herself that he had caught her in a weak moment. What was driving her was the almost painful clawing heat of sheer sexual hunger and the awareness shocked her.

'We shouldn't,' she told him weakly, even as her hand rose to his face and her fingers traced the splendid angle of one high cheekbone, her thumb stroking along the edge of his beautiful mouth, which was capable of giving her so much pleasure.

'Let's not go back to the games we used to play before we got married, *mi dulzura*,' Alejandro husked in sensual reproof.

Utterly bewildered by that comment, Jemima dropped her hand and stared up at him. 'What are you trying to imply...?'

CHAPTER SIX

'No COMMITMENT, no sex,' Alejandro paraphrased huskily. 'You utilised the most basic feminine weapon of all.'

'That wasn't a game or a weapon!' Jemima protested in a pained voice, wounded that he could even think that of her. From the moment she'd realised just how strong a hold Alejandro had on her heart, she had tried her best to protect herself. Saying no to sex while he still had other women in his bed had seemed to be common sense rather than a form of manipulation.

'Why pretend?' Alejandro murmured, lowering his handsome dark head and letting his jaw line rasp softly along the extended line of her throat before he followed that trail with his mouth, lingering in places that became erogenous just through his touch and laughing when she squirmed beneath him. 'It was highly effective. In the end I wanted you, *only* you. I wanted you so much that having you began to seem like winning the top prize. And I have to admit, you more than lived up to your promise in my bed.'

Her cheeks flushed. 'But it wasn't a game. It might've been for you, it wasn't for me. I was a virgin, for goodness' sake!'

'And I was duly appreciative of the fact. I married you,' Alejandro reminded her doggedly.

But Jemima had just had an unsettling glimpse into how he viewed those months prior to their marriage. Evidently he had always believed that it was the power of lust for her long-withheld body that had stoked his desire to the point where he offered her a wedding ring so that she was always around, always available. With that shallow basis, was it any wonder that their relationship had failed? There was nothing lasting about lust, she told herself, even as she lifted her hips in a helpless circling motion beneath the pressure of his weight on hers, every skin cell singing with eagerness.

Alejandro shimmied down her body to let his mouth travel across the pale hillocks of her breasts encased in turquoise silk and lace cups. He released the catch on her bra and tugged her up against him to enjoy the warm soft weight of the sensitive flesh that spilled into his hands. She gasped as he entrapped the straining peaks between thumb and finger, rubbing the swollen pink tips until she leant back into him with an uninhibited moan of response.

'I love your breasts,' he husked. 'Such a delightfully lush surprise on that tiny frame of yours.'

Jemima strained back against him, her spine arching as the feeling of pressure and awareness low in her pelvis increased. He twisted her round and down again and found the delicate rosy buds he had already massaged into prominence with his devouring mouth. It was as though her breasts were a hotline to her groin, for the surge of heat and moisture between her thighs was instantaneous. A finger stroked along the taut damp band of fabric at her crotch and she flinched, letting her head fall back as a low moan of encouragement was wrenched from her throat. She wanted him so much it hurt to wait.

'Have you any idea how often I've fantasised about this moment in the last few weeks?' Alejandro asked her thickly, peeling off her panties and using a knee to part her legs. His dark golden eyes glowed with sexual heat over the naked expanse of her delicate curves.

Jemima was trembling. The temptation to revel in the depth of his desire had died on the reflection that lust had no longevity and lying willingly naked for his appraisal only made her all the more conscious of the things she didn't like about her body. She had always thought that her legs were too short and the extra weight she carried at breast and hip too much for her height. As she began to curl away from him he bent down and crushed her lips under his with a passionate urgency that burned through her like a flaming brand. The plunge of his tongue affected her like a chain of firecrackers sparking through her taut length and her hips rose pleadingly, her whole body singing with sharp urgent need.

'Oh, *please*,' she said shakily, impatient, needy, wanting more than she could bear.

'I want to enjoy you first…I want to wait,' Alejandro framed with ragged ardour, playing with the delicate pearly folds between her thighs while he worked his skilful passage down over her quivering body, watching her expressive face as she fought to stay in control.

'Don't watch me,' she urged unevenly, suffering sweet torment from the hunger he was stoking.

He touched her with such infinite finesse, knowing the perfect spot, the exact amount of pressure, the ideal pace. She cried out loud, eyelashes sliding down to screen her eyes as the pleasure raced and screamed through her twisting length. He licked the skin of her inner thigh, following the trail to a more intimate place and dallying there with sensual expertise until she thought she might pass out with the intensity of her response. Her climax took her like a roaring storm, demanding every ounce of her energy and throwing her up to a breathless height of excruciating pleasure as she writhed in sobbing satisfaction.

He pulled back from her when she wanted him to hold her close. The world was a thousand miles away from her at that moment when she was still lost in the cocoon of all that breathtaking pleasure. Then she heard the slide of a drawer, the sound of foil tearing and a moment later he was back with her. After what she said earlier, she registered that he would not risk her falling pregnant again.

Jemima felt wanton, because when he came back to her he was hugely aroused and her body thrilled anew for she could hardly wait for that final act of possession. Orgasm hadn't satisfied that deep driving need to be with him again in the most basic way of all. He slid over her and she lifted to him at the first probing thrust of his bold shaft. He felt so big, so good when he plunged into her long and hard and deep and she gasped, violet eyes flying wide, raw excitement licking through her like flames.

'You *really* want me,' Alejandro growled with all-male satisfaction, surging into her receptive body with sudden driving urgency.

It was like being caught in the eye of a hurricane. A kind of stormy wildness pulsed through her to stoke the rising rush of crazy excitement already leaping high with her anticipation. Alejandro settled on a potent pagan rhythm. He was rampant, irresistible and her heartbeat thumped faster and faster in tune with his strong movements. Gasping, she rose under him, her body moving of its own accord as the feverish, hot, stimulating delight of his possession gave her ever-increasing pleasure. Somewhere towards the end of that ravenous ride she screamed, writhing as the ecstatic convulsions of a second climax seized hold of her. The sheer intensity of the experience almost made her black out and she lay shell shocked in the aftermath.

'*Dios mio*. That was amazing,' Alejandro husked above her head, his arms still anchored round her to keep her close. 'To think that I was afraid I might not be able to get it up with you because of Marco. You deliver such an erotic buzz I would have to be made of stone to resist you.'

Jemima tensed and stiffened defensively. Her lips parted and almost simultaneously a long brown forefinger nudged against her mouth.

'No more denials, *querida*. Every time you deny what you did I get angry again and it has been a very long and difficult day,' Alejandro admitted heavily.

Prevented from stating her case by his wall of entrenched disbelief and distrust, Jemima suffered an immediate sense of alienation and she pulled free of his embrace to roll over into a cooler spot in the bed. She lay on her side and looked back at him, her violet eyes bright with antagonism below her wildly tumbled strawberry-blonde curls. He looked so relaxed, black hair tousled by her fingers above his bold bronzed profile. Her fair skin was tingling and probably pink from the burn of the stubble he hadn't got to shave off before taking her to bed, but deep down inside her there was a well of indescribable physical satisfaction that had been running on empty ever since she had left Spain previously. Their marriage had always been a blazing success in the bedroom. But she knew it would be a long time before she got over the embarrassment of having revealed just how much she had craved his touch.

Alejandro turned his handsome head on the pillow to look at her with spectacular dark brown eyes semi-veiled by lush ebony lashes. 'Surely you can see that we cannot make a success of living together again without an honest acceptance of the past?'

Her generous mouth took on a mutinous slant. He had already travelled from refusing to believe her to refusing even to *listen* to her denials so what hope of exoneration did that give her for the future? His belief in her infidelity was unshakable.

'Shower, then dinner,' Alejandro instructed arrogantly in the smouldering silence, closing a stubborn hand over hers to drag her across to his side of the bed while he tossed back the sheet and vaulted upright.

'Where were you today? What happened that you had to leave a message for me?' Jemima asked abruptly as he propelled her into the spacious bathroom with him.

'Pepe, one of the vineyard workers, had a tractor accident. He was badly hurt,' Alejandro told her, his mouth compressing into a bleak line. 'I stayed at the hospital to support his wife. Their only child lives abroad and the other relatives are elderly. I'm afraid Pepe didn't make it and by the time I got his wife home again and offered my condolences to the rest of the family…'

Jemima was aghast at what he was telling her. 'Yes,

I can imagine how awful it must have been. I'm sorry, if I'd known I wouldn't have said anything—'

'But you didn't know so you were entitled to complain.' The speed with which he dismissed the matter told her that he didn't want to discuss it further. He had not exaggerated when he had said what a difficult day he'd had.

In the spacious tiled shower with the water streaming down over his big bronzed body he leant back against the wall for a moment or two, his eyes closing, and she finally appreciated just how tired he was. Her conscience smote her and she resented that feeling because when they were first married Alejandro had often contrived to make her feel that way. So often he'd had something more important, serious or meaningful to do with his time than be with her. She had often felt guilty, undeserving or selfish for just wanting to see more of him. Pepe's wife and family, however, would have found his presence a source of great comfort and support because he was that kind of a guy: strong and reliable in times of crisis.

Knowing that, she had often wondered why he had let her down so badly when she needed him. Or as his unsuitable and unhappy wife had she simply been yet another burden and source of worry for him, one he'd been relieved to be free of again? It would be foolish for her to forget that he had only taken her back so that he could have his son living with him in his home in Spain.

She didn't bother getting dressed again. Clad in a blue nightdress and satin wrap, she joined Alejandro in the reception room adjoining their bedroom where a meal was served in spite of the late hour. Casually clad in jeans and a black T-shirt, he looked younger and more approachable as well as heart-stoppingly handsome. A big vase of fresh white daisies adorned the round table and she remembered how his mother had once summarily dumped one of Jemima's own amateur floral arrangements. In those days she had been naïve, easily hurt and upset. She had barely had the maturity to be a wife, never mind a mother, and she had made more than one stupid decision, opting for the wrong choices and what had seemed like the easy way out when life got tough.

Alejandro studied his reclaimed wife intently across the table. Even with her pale hair in an untidy riot of curls and without a scrap of make-up, she was so beautiful with her fragile features, flawless skin and unusually coloured eyes that she commanded and held his full attention. The sex might be even more amazing than he recalled but he wasn't yet fully convinced that he had her where he wanted and needed her to be. The memory of her three-month proviso outraged his sense of justice. His polar opposite, she was impulsive, capricious and, as he had cause to know, wildly extravagant. It would be a challenge to predict her next move.

Once again he was at war with himself, Alejandro recognised angrily. It was a familiar predicament where Jemima was concerned. How could he have so compromised his convictions that he took back an unfaithful wife? Moreover, an unfaithful wife who still refused to admit her guilt? And an unrepentant gold-digger who had undoubtedly only survived in England for so long without his financial support because she had already carefully bled him dry of thousands of euros before she'd left him. Her escape fund? What else? It was a galling suspicion for a male once accustomed to female adulation and pursuit. Only his wife had run in the other direction.

But what right had he to the moral high ground? He had used their toddler son as a weapon and blackmailed her into returning yet, amazingly, he didn't feel guilty about what he had done. Had he not acted in his son's best interests? Dealing with such a woman demanded extraordinary measures.

He sipped his wine, savouring the vintage while his keen intelligence continued to present him with truths he would have preferred to ignore. Jemima might make him burn with desire but she was bad news for him. A man should aspire to a decent woman with standards, not stoop to the level of a dishonourable and deceitful one. But the instant he'd been subjected to the sight of the men panting after her skirts in that little English village his libido and territorial instincts had flamed to unmanageable heights. The prospect of leaving her free to take such men to her bed in his place had sentenced him to sleepless nights and repeated cold showers, for his blood ran hot.

Jemima was *his* and, undeniably, a weakness. Every man could afford an indulgence as long as he practised damage control, Alejandro ruminated, his lean, strong face hard with self-discipline. And she couldn't hurt him because he didn't love her. He had never been in love and was proud of the fact, he reminded himself with innate pride. Men in love were fools with women while a man in lust knew exactly what he was doing and why he was doing it.

Uncomfortable with the lingering silence, Jemima finally spoke up. 'There were reporters and cameras at the airport when I arrived for my flight out here today. They seemed to be waiting for Alfie and me, expecting us…'

Alejandro was frowning with annoyance. 'Someone

must have tipped them off. How else would they have known you would be there?'

'Well, it wasn't me—'

'Are you sure of that?' Alejandro prompted cynically.

Her eyes widened in surprise and consternation. 'But why would I tip off the paparazzi?'

'Either because you were paid for the information or because you revel in the attention of the press.' Alejandro tossed his napkin down and rose to his full impressive height. His devastatingly handsome features were grave. 'Whichever it is, be warned: I don't like that kind of publicity.'

'Where are you going?' Jemima pressed tautly, already reeling from the accusation he had just made.

'To bed. I'll look in on Alfie first. *Buenas noches, querida.*'

A faint surge of pink illuminated her delicate bone structure. Her hands clenched into fists of restraint below the level of the table but she passed no further comment. After their passionate lovemaking in what had once been the marital bed his departure for the night to a separate room was like a slap in the face. It was a reminder that appearances were deceptive and that neither the expensive gift of a new wardrobe nor the meal eaten *à deux* meant that they were engaged in a genuine reconciliation.

'I didn't tell the paps that we were getting back together,' Jemima declared loudly.

'Someone did.' Unimpressed dark golden eyes clashed with hers, his strong jaw line at an aggressive angle.

'You know, I didn't appreciate you taking on a nanny without discussing it with me first,' she confided abruptly, deciding that she might as well confront that issue.

'We can discuss that tomorrow,' Alejandro fielded impatiently and a moment later he was gone, leaving her still seated with her dessert sitting untouched in front of her.

Minutes later, the maid arrived with a trolley to clear the table and Jemima went to check on her son, finding him sound asleep in his cot. For a moment she envied the contentment etched in Alfie's peaceful little face. A strange cot in an unfamiliar room and new faces all around him? No problem. Alejandro's son had rolled with the punches and he saw no reason to stay awake and on guard. And why shouldn't her son feel that way? There could be no comparison between his childhood and the one his mother had endured, which had marked her all her life with fear and anxiety. Alfie's world had always been safe and his needs had always been met. He had never been denied love. He had never known violence or malice. And Jemima was quietly proud of the fact that she had done much more for him than her parents had ever done for her.

Back in the bedroom she slid into bed and put on the television, finally tuning into a music channel before resting back against the pillows.

She had no idea what time it was when a sound wakened her and she half sat up, pushing her hair out of her eyes and blinking as Alejandro flicked the remote control at the television to switch it off. The bedside lamp was still lit. 'I must've fallen asleep,' she mumbled drowsily, wondering if the noise from the set had disturbed him, for he was barefoot and wearing only his jeans with the top button undone. A silky black furrow of hair ran down over his stomach and disappeared below the waistband. Suddenly she felt hot.

Alejandro sent her a brooding look from glittering dark eyes. 'I'm sleeping here tonight,' he informed her with a hostile stare-you-down cool stamped on his lean dark features as though he expected her to argue with him.

Jemima was startled by that announcement. After all, it was already three in the morning according to the digital display on the clock by the bed. Lips parting slowly in surprise, Jemima watched as he shed his jeans. A lean, powerfully muscular silhouette—he was wearing, it transpired, not a stitch below the denim and he was…well, he *was* sporting a rampant erection. There was really no avoiding that fact. Hot colour washed her face and a melted-honey sensation curled low in her pelvis. She was his object of desire and he couldn't hide it and she liked that. The separate-bedroom concept had bitten the dust at remarkable speed.

'I should be too tired for this, *querida*,' Alejandro growled as he came down on the bed beside her, his every fluid movement full of virile masculine promise. 'But I can't sleep for wanting you.'

Jemima lay back like Cleopatra reclining on a ceremonial barge, ever ready to be admired. She gazed up at him in sultry invitation and with hot golden eyes he crushed her soft full mouth under his with an erotic savagery that sent desire lancing through her slim length in an arrow of fire. She closed her hand round him and he shifted against her with a guttural sound while she teased the silky sleek heat of his sex over its iron-hard core. With an eagerness that thrilled her, he wrenched her free of the nightdress, his hands finding the white globes of her breasts and then the swollen damp flesh between her thighs. Every sense on high alert, her body went wild as the pounding throb of heat and hunger pulsed through her tender body, racking her with a stark storm of need.

'*Por Dios*, I can't wait,' Alejandro framed hungrily through a welter of passionate and devouring kisses that only left her gasping for more.

And dimly Jemima wondered what was happening to her because, somehow, even though she had been satiated he had set her alight again and the balance of power was no longer hers. Alejandro had never felt more necessary to her as he turned her on her side and plunged into her tight hot core, stretching her, filling her with a sweet, dominant force she could not resist. Delirious excitement powered through her quivering body in wave after wave when he rubbed her swollen nipples and teased the tiny bud of pleasure below her mound. He pounded into her at an enthralling pace until the ache and the burn combined into a fiery explosion. She reached a shattering release, convulsive spasms of delight roaring through her sobbing, shaking length until at last she lay still in his arms, weak and utterly spent.

Alejandro turned her round and pressed a kiss to her cheek before stretching up to douse the lights. 'Nobody but you has ever given me pleasure like that.'

And in receipt of that accolade, Jemima went from warm and reassured into a place of wounding self-doubt. Nothing had changed. It was always all about sex as far as Alejandro was concerned. He had never loved her yet, even though she had never believed she was the wife he really wanted, he had still married her. That had never made sense to her. But even so, Jemima was all too used to not making the grade with those she loved. Her mother would have loved and valued her daughter more had Jemima been the baby boy she had wanted to please her husband. Her father had never loved her, nor had he ever pretended to. There had been boyfriends but no one serious before Alejandro and she had fallen so hard for him that the sheer pain of having once loved and lost him still had the power to wound her.

She lay awake in the darkness, reassured by his continuing presence. It might only be sex that kept him there but that was better than nothing, wasn't it? She could walk away from him again without getting hurt, she told herself soothingly. She didn't love him any more; she had got over that nonsense. Once she had believed that Marco's obvious pleasure in her company might magically make his big brother view his wife with newly appreciative eyes. Instead Alejandro had simply assumed that her close friendship with Marco was based on sex. When that was the only tie he himself acknowledged with her, how could he have understood that she and Marco had bonded on quite another level?

Suppressing a regretful sigh over her tangled and unhappy past, Jemima finally drifted off to sleep...

CHAPTER SEVEN

JEMIMA only awoke when china rattled on a tray and the curtains were trailed noisily back. Sunlight drenched the bed in a shower of warm golden brilliance and she sat up with a sleepy sigh. She was immediately conscious of the stiffness of her limbs and the intimate ache at the heart of her. X-rated memories of how she had celebrated the breaking of the dawn assailed her. It was little wonder she had slept like a log afterwards, not even stirring when Alejandro got up.

She stared in disbelief at her watch, for the day was in full swing and it was comfortably past noon. The maid set down the tray on a side table and settled Jemima's wrap down on the bed for her use while asking her whether she wanted to eat in the room next door or outside on the roof terrace. Self-conscious at being naked, with her nightdress lying in a heap in the middle of the floor where Alejandro had hurled it, Jemima fought her way into the wrap while contriving to stay mostly covered by the sheet.

'Thanks. I'll eat outside,' she said, sliding out of bed and pushing her feet into mules to follow the maid through the door and up the little narrow curving staircase in the corner and out onto the roof terrace of the tower. Once it had been her favourite place in the castle, safe from all intruders and prying eyes. Warm, all-encompassing heat curled round her lightly clad frame when she stepped out into the fresh air to enjoy the magnificent view she remembered. It stretched as far as the eye could see right up to the snow-capped Sierra Mountains that girded the valley.

Far below in the gardens she heard a child's laughter and she stood at the battlements from where she espied Alfie, who was playing ball on an immaculate green lawn with a small figure she assumed to be Placida. Some mother she had proved to be since her arrival at the castle, she reflected ruefully. Resolving to spend the rest of the day with him, Jemima sat down at the shaded table and quickly embarked on the delicious lunch on the tray. She was really hungry and ate with appetite before taking the tray back downstairs, laying out white cropped knee-length trousers and a green T-shirt from her own store to wear and heading straight for the shower.

Her hair in damp ringlets, she was coming down the main staircase when she heard a female voice raised in shrill argument. Indeed the voice might almost have been described as being at screaming pitch and it was matched by the deep bass notes of a clipped male voice. The racket was emanating from the imposing salon on the ground floor. In the main hall two of the domestic staff were stationed outside the service door to the kitchens and clearly engaged in eavesdropping. Her face flushed and miserable, Beatriz emerged abruptly from the room and the staff slipped hurriedly through the service door and out of sight.

'What's going on?' Jemima asked baldly.

'*Mamá* is very offended with Alejandro,' Beatriz told her uncomfortably.

'Oh…' Stifling her curiosity because she thought it wiser not to get involved in a family matter, Jemima walked right past the door of the salon. 'I'm going out to the garden to join Alfie and Placida.'

Alejandro's sister accompanied her, clearly keen to escape the bad feeling on the domestic front. 'Alejandro has asked Doña Hortencia to move into a house on the estate,' she revealed.

Startled by that news, Jemima turned to look at her companion with wide eyes of enquiry. 'My goodness, that's very sudden!'

'Her belongings are already being packed,' Beatriz declared in a dazed undertone. '*Mamá* is very shocked. I have never seen Alejandro so angry or so resolute. She is to move into a hotel until the house is fully prepared for her.'

'That must have been some argument.' Jemima did not have the hypocrisy to pretend regret at the prospect of Doña Hortencia moving out of the castle, but she was very much surprised by the development.

'I will miss my nephew,' Alejandro's sister admitted heavily.

'But surely you're not moving out as well?' Jemima exclaimed.

'*Mamá* will expect me to accompany her.'

'But I don't and I'm sure Alejandro won't either,' Jemima stated, because she knew that Alejandro was very fond of his sister and troubled by the restricted life she led with their mother. 'This has always been your home, Beatriz.'

The tall, full-figured brunette lifted worried eyes to hers. 'Are you sure that you and Alejandro wouldn't mind if I stayed on?'

'Of course, we wouldn't. I would be glad of your company, particularly when Alejandro is away on business.'

'My stepmother would never forgive me for deserting her...' Beatriz looked shocked at the concept of the new way of life she was clearly envisaging. 'I'm not sure I *could* go against her wishes and do it—'

Her brow pleating, Jemima had come to a sudden halt. 'Did you just refer to Doña Hortencia as your "step-mother"? Or did I get that wrong?'

In her turn, Beatriz frowned uncertainly at the smaller blonde woman. 'Didn't you know?' she queried somewhat abstractedly, her mind clearly still focused on her future living arrangements. 'Of course we have always had to call her *Mamá*. I was only three years old and Alejandro a newborn baby when our own mother died.'

Jemima stifled the curious questions ready to spring to her lips. It was typical that Alejandro had not chosen to enlighten her as to that salient fact. It did at least explain why Doña Hortencia had always seemed very cold towards her elder son while seeming almost dotingly fond of his younger brother, Marco. 'But Marco is?'

'Marco was born four years after Doña Hortencia married our father,' Beatriz confirmed quietly. '*Mamá* was very upset when she realised that Marco could not inherit a larger portion of what our father left in his will because it would have meant splitting up and selling the estate.'

Alfie ran across the lawn to throw himself at his mother when he saw her approaching. Laughing and cuddling his solid little body, Jemima hugged her son close and urged his nanny to take a break. Beatriz played ball with her nephew and Jemima found herself hoping that her sister-in-law would have the courage to break free of her stepmother's suffocating control and stay on at the castle.

Almost an hour later, Alejandro strolled out to join them. Sheathed in lightweight khaki chinos with the sleek lines of a designer fit and a short-sleeved shirt, he looked gorgeous. When his spectacular black spiky-lashed golden gaze sought hers, Jemima went pink as she recalled the intimacies they had shared so freely during the night hours. Alfie beamed at his father and gave him the ball while Beatriz excused herself, saying that she ought to go and see if she could assist Doña Hortencia.

Jemima stood by containing her intense curiosity while Alejandro and Alfie fooled about with the ball. When they had both had enough, Alejandro suggested taking Alfie down to the lake and loaded them into an estate vehicle.

'I didn't realise until Beatriz mentioned it that Doña Hortencia was actually your stepmother.'

Alejandro compressed his lips. 'She's the only mother I can remember. My own died from eclampsia within hours of my birth.'

'That was a tragic loss for all of you,' Jemima remarked.

'My father remarried months after her death. Hortencia, not my mother, was the true love of his life,' Alejandro explained flatly. 'He worshipped the ground she walked on and he came close to bankrupting the estate in his determination to give her the very best of everything.'

Jemima was suddenly beginning to revise her once sunny assumptions about Alejandro's childhood. 'Was it a happy marriage?'

'*He* was happy, but I don't think she has ever been satisfied in her life with what she had. When my father was dying, however, he became very concerned about Hortencia's future—I believe she had shared her fears with him—and he begged me to always treat her as though she was my birth mother. It was his last wish. I gave my word and I have respected it ever since. Until today it did not occur to me that in tolerating her excesses I had been unfair to you.'

'Why?' Jemima questioned. 'What happened today?'

'Had you let me know how my stepmother was treating you when we were first married I would have stopped it then. You should have been honest with me,' Alejandro murmured in a tone of reproach rather than censure, his striking eyes troubled. 'This was your home and as my wife it is your right to take charge of the castle and the staff—'

'I'm not sure I could have coped with the responsibility in those days,' Jemima cut in lightly, realising that for some inexplicable reason all she wanted to do at that moment was make him feel better rather than add another weight to his conscience.

His lean, strong face clenched hard. 'But you never had the opportunity to *try*. Had you not been hampered by Hortencia's spite you would have managed perfectly well. You are a capable young woman.'

'Did your sister say that she was spiteful?' Jemima prompted in surprise, for Beatriz virtually never had a bad word to say about anyone. They were walking down towards the lake that gleamed through a grove of silvery olive trees like a reflective mirror on the valley floor.

A brooding expression darkened Alejandro's features. 'There was no need for her to do so. The manner in which my stepmother spoke of you today was sufficient for me to appreciate the level of malice which I was dealing with. The only possible solution was for her to move out—'

'Do you regret that?'

'How could I?' Alejandro confided with a harsh laugh that acknowledged the older woman's challenging temperament. 'Although Beatriz and I had no choice but to treat her as our mother, she had no maternal love to give us. She sent both of us off to boarding school as soon as she could. And after Marco was born, she resented my position as the eldest son and ensured that I had little contact with my father.'

'Then you were kinder to her than she deserved,' Jemima pronounced feelingly.

'But I can't forgive myself for not appreciating how she was treating you when I first made this your home.' Alejandro stared down at her with intent eyes and reached for her hand in a warm gesture of encouragement that took her by surprise. 'I hope you can move past that bad beginning now and learn to love this place and its people as I do, *querida*.'

That he wanted things to change for her benefit and that he had already made a bold first move towards that end pleased Jemima a great deal. But it was the eloquent expression in those beautiful eyes the colour of rich malt whisky in sunlight that affected her the most. He really did want their marriage to work this time around and, even though that might be primarily because they now had a child to consider, his determination and his caring about what it would take to make her happy in

Spain impressed her. It was a beginning, and a better beginning than they had made together when they first married...

A slight figure in an emerald-green silk skirt suit that was bright against her fair complexion and wealth of strawberry-blonde hair, Jemima stepped up to the podium with a heart beating as fast as a drum. She set her little prompt card down where it could catch her eye if she forgot what she had to say. As this was her first ever public speech, she had kept it short and succinct and had rehearsed it thoroughly with Beatriz beforehand.

In spite of those precautions, though, perspiration still dampened her short upper lip and her nerves were bouncing about like jumping beans. At a nod of readiness from the charity director, Jemima began to speak about the need for the sanctuary for female victims of domestic violence being provided by the shelter. The fund-raising benefit was aimed at providing new purpose-built premises where women and children could stay in safety and begin to rebuild their lives.

At the back of function room, she was conscious of Alejandro watching her. Beatriz was by her brother's side and smiling encouragement, but it was less easy to tell what Alejandro was thinking. She was pleased enough that he had rescheduled a business trip so that he could accompany her to the evening event. Jemima returned to their table, quietly content that she had contrived to control her nerves. It was thanks to Beatriz, who had long had an interest in the charity, that Jemima had got involved. Although it was not a fact that she would have shared with her husband, she had felt a great sense of empathy with the frightened women and children she had met and talked to at the shelter.

'You were terrific, *esposa mia*.' Alejandro regarded her with frank approbation and she reached for his hand to squeeze it. He had just called her his wife in a tone of pride and affection that went a long way towards healing the still raw wounds inflicted in the past.

But then, over the past couple of months Jemima had seen a different side to Alejandro's brooding temperament. As he turned his handsome head and stood up to politely acknowledge the greeting of a local businessman she was wearing a warm smile. Somehow they had put the past away, although sometimes she feared that putting those troubles untouched into a locked box was more of a shortcut than a long term solution. Marco was never, ever mentioned and neither, fortunately, she felt, was the disturbing question of all the money she had once contrived to run through.

On the other hand, she and Alejandro were enjoying an accord that they had never had in the past when he worked such long hours that she was constantly left to her own devices and deprived of a social life. It was that isolation that had made her so grateful for Marco's friendliness. But over two years on Alejandro had learned how to make time for her and Alfie and he had made the effort to introduce them to his world. He had taken them over every inch of the valley, showing them over his various businesses and introducing them to the tenants and the employees, so that for the first time Jemima felt as though the estate and the castle were her home as well.

An opening day for the public to view the castle had given Jemima the excuse to do several floral arrangements. Family, friends and relations, who had attended a dinner party that same evening, had been hugely impressed and Jemima had already received several requests to act as a floral consultant at local events. Having acted as an advisor at a couple now, she wasn't yet sure that she wanted to embark on what promised to be another business. No longer subject to Doña Hortencia's withering asides and cutting put-downs, Jemima was comfortable entertaining guests at the castle and had discovered that just being herself was sufficient.

Day by day, Alfie was blossoming; his days were much more active and varied than they had been in Charlbury St Helens and there were far more people around to give him attention. In fact, for a while, all that admiring attention had rather gone to Alfie's head and he had become too demanding; a solid week of toddler tantrums had ensued whenever he'd been subjected to the word no. Jemima had been amused by the discovery that Alejandro, so tough in other ways, had had to steel himself to be firm with his son when the little boy had thrown himself on the ground and sobbed with a drama that she was convinced came from his father's side of the family. It was a new relationship for Alejandro, who had never been allowed to enjoy the same close ties with his own father as a boy.

And so far Alejandro had shown every sign of being a brilliant dad. He had put a lot of effort into building a good relationship with his little son. Alfie adored him and raced to greet him the minute he heard his footsteps or his voice. Jemima had been impressed by the time and trouble Alejandro had taken to get to know Alfie and find out what he enjoyed. She had only to see father and son together to know that she had made the right decision in coming back to Spain.

Jemima was also happy in a way she had never thought she could be again, although sometimes she felt as if she were floating in a deceptively calm sea while wilfully ignoring the dangerous undertow and the concealed rocks. The next day, Alejandro took her on a long drive through the mountains to a sleepy town with an amazing little restaurant that served astonishingly good food. As they were getting back into the car Alejandro asked without the smallest warning, 'Did Marco ever bring you up here?'

And caught unawares with her defences down, she felt her face freeze, wasn't able to help that strong reaction to a name that was never voiced. 'No, he didn't. I would have said,' she murmured stiffly.

Clearly unimpressed by that claim, Alejandro gave her a hard dark appraisal, which warned her that though the body of her supposed infidelity might have been buried it was still at great risk of being disinterred. He hadn't forgotten or forgiven her imaginary betrayal and, for several taut seconds while she gazed stonily back at him, she bristled with an amount of resentment and rancour that would go a fair way to destroying any marital reconciliation. It was a struggle to keep the lid on her emotions.

'I shouldn't have asked,' Alejandro conceded tautly, the two of them momentarily enclosed by the suffocating sweaty heat of the car before the air conditioning could kick in and cool the interior.

'I'm surprised you did—Marco has urban tastes. He prefers clubs and culture to the countryside,' Jemima reminded him, staring fixedly out through the windscreen but seeing nothing, wondering why she had said that, why she had extended the dialogue instead of dropping it cold.

'And you always did like dancing,' Alejandro quipped, his intonation stinging like a sharp needle jabbed in the arm.

'After we were married, when did you ever take me?' Jemima countered defiantly, ready and looking for a fight now, all patience at an end.

Brilliant dark golden eyes alight with scorching rebuke at that tart gibe, Alejandro closed long brown fingers round her hand to tug her closer and he brought his mouth hotly and hungrily down on hers in retribution. For an instant her hand skimmed down over one high olive cheekbone in an unintended caress and then she dropped her hand and her fingers closed into the front of his jacket and clenched there instead, because the burning stream of desire he had unleashed fired her up as fiercely as her disturbed emotions. Her breasts were taut nubs below her clothing, the tender flesh between her thighs warm and moist and ready. Swearing only half under his breath at the intensity of her response, Alejandro thrust her back from him and started up the car.

'You shouldn't begin anything you can't finish,' she whispered helplessly, her body stabbing her with jagged regret over the loss of that so necessary physical contact with him.

Without warning Alejandro laughed and shot her a wicked long-lashed glance, his wide sensual mouth curling with amusement. 'I have every intention of finishing what I began, *tesora mia.*'

'It will take us well over an hour just to get home,' Jemima reminded him.

But only a few minutes later, Alejandro turned his Ferrari off the road and drew up outside a country hotel. She turned startled eyes on him. 'You can't be serious?'

'Only an acrobat could have good sex in this car,' Alejandro fielded, vaulting out and striding round the bonnet to open the passenger seat door and extract her.

'But we've got no luggage!' she protested in a panicked undertone, colouring hotly with self-consciousness when he strode over to the reception desk, his dark head held high, and asked for a room without the smallest hint of discomfiture.

'Your face is too well known. People will get to know about this,' she muttered ruefully when the door closed behind the porter and left them alone in a well-appointed room. Yet even as she sounded that note of caution she was excited by his audacity and his single-minded pursuit of satisfaction.

An unholy grin lit Alejandro's lean, darkly handsome features as he reached for her again. 'After imbibing a little too freely of the wine we had with lunch I was falling asleep at the wheel and rather than risk continuing our journey I did the sensible thing and took a break,' he mocked.

'The famous Spanish siesta, much written about but more rarely found in practice these days,' she teased.

'I promise that you will enjoy every moment of our siesta, *querida*,' Alejandro swore with a husky growl of anticipation edging his deep dark drawl.

And then he kissed her, and the heat and the craving

gripped her again with even greater power. He stripped off her clothes between passionate breathless kisses and she fought with his shirt buttons and his belt, already wildly, feverishly aware of the rigid fullness of his erection. She sank down on her knees and used her mouth on him until his hands closed tightly into her hair to restrain her and he was trembling against her.

He hauled her back up to him and tumbled her down on the crisp white linen sheets that awaited them. There was no need of further foreplay for either of them. He sank into her long and slow and deep and she quivered on a sexual high of intense response and so it continued until she hit a soul-shattering climax and her body convulsed in sweet spasms of delight around him.

'You can go to sleep now if you like,' Jemima whispered generously with a voluptuous stretch in the aftermath.

Laughing, Alejandro cradled her close and claimed another kiss. 'I have a much better idea.'

Jemima smiled, loving that physical closeness and relaxation and the charismatic smile tugging at the corners of his mouth as he gazed down at her. And suddenly new awareness of her emotions struck like an electric shock pulsing through her brain. Her eyes veiled when she registered that she could no longer imagine returning to England to live and work, could not picture herself ever leaving him again, indeed could not face the prospect of such a separation. Yet hadn't they both agreed to a three-month trial, which would very soon be up?

Although she had only been back in Spain with Alejandro for a brief period it had taken him a remarkably short time to break through her defensive barriers. She had started looking for him whenever he wasn't there, counting the hours when he was away from her until he was back again and within reach. She was falling for him all over again, she reflected worriedly, falling back in love with a guy who could only be programmed to hurt her for as long as he still believed that she had slept with his kid brother.

'What's up?' Alejandro queried, feeling her tension and lifting his tousled dark head to look down into her face with a frown.

'Nothing,' she swore, pushing close again, turning her lips up to his again and offering sex as a means of distraction.

And because Alejandro was and always had been a very passionate man, it worked a treat. There were no more awkward questions and there was an astounding amount of lovemaking until eventually they both drifted off to sleep exhausted. After dining at the hotel, they arrived back at the castle at quite a late hour. Maria, the housekeeper, greeted Jemima with the news that an Englishman had rung twice asking for her but had not left his name for her to call back.

Jemima had no idea who could have been calling her, for virtually all her connections back in England were female. 'Are you sure it was a man?' And at Maria's nod of confirmation, she shrugged and remarked, 'If it's important he'll ring back again.'

While she talked to the older woman, Beatriz had emerged from the salon and was speaking to her brother. Her sister-in-law's usual ready smile was absent and before Jemima's eyes Alejandro's stance transformed from relaxed to tense.

'Did something happen while we were out?' Jemima enquired when Beatriz hurried away again.

Alejandro settled his forbidding dark gaze on her, his lean bronzed face all Renaissance Man angles and hollows in the shadows cast by the wall lights, his jaw line as set as though it were carved from stone. 'Marco's come home for a visit. He's staying with his mother.'

And having dropped that bombshell, Alejandro said something flat about having work to do and, before she could part her lips, he was gone and she was standing alone in the echoing stone hall...

CHAPTER EIGHT

MARCO was back! It seemed a surprising coincidence that Alejandro's brother should choose to make his first visit home in years so soon after her own return to Spain. Jemima tossed and turned in her bed, unable to sleep while her thoughts ran on at a mad frantic pitch and refused to give her peace. She wondered too where Alejandro was and if he was really working.

Alejandro was less than pleased by news of his brother's arrival. Guilt squirmed through Jemima as she could remember when Alejandro was very fond of his younger brother and, whether she liked it or not, she had played an unwitting part in their estrangement. With hindsight, however, she recognised that Marco's feelings for his elder brother had always been less clear-cut. Idolised and spoiled by both parents as the baby of the family, Marco had nonetheless competed all his life within Alejandro's shadow and had never equalled or surpassed his sibling's achievements. Athletically gifted and academically brilliant, Alejandro had outshone Marco without effort and had set a bar that Marco could not reach. Even in business, Alejandro had triumphed while Marco had failed as an independent businessman and had eventually settled for a tailor-made position running one of the art galleries in his brother's empire.

But, those facts notwithstanding, Jemima had got on like a house on fire with Marco from the moment she had met him. Not that back then Marco had had much competition, since although Alejandro had been a brand-new husband at the time he had also been a workaholic and Jemima had been lonely, bored and unhappy. In the stiflingly formal household that Doña Hortencia had insisted on then, Marco had seemed like a breath of fresh air and Jemima had quickly warmed to her brother-in-law's light-hearted charm. In those days she had been blind to the reality that Marco might have a darker side to his nature than he had ever shown her.

How else could Marco have sacrificed a friendship with Jemima that he had once sworn meant a great deal to him? How else could he have allowed Alejandro to go on believing that his wife had slept with his brother? Why on earth had Marco done that? How could he have been so cruel and callous towards his brother and his former friend? She still didn't understand and *needed* to know the answer to those questions. What she did know was that Marco had gone to New York and embarked on a new life there, seemingly indifferent to the chaos and unhappiness he had left in his wake.

But while Jemima lay there ruminating on the past anger began to smoulder deep down inside her. Why was she feeling guilty about someone else's lies and another person's refusal to believe in her word? Marco was the one who had lied, at the very least by omission, and as a result Alejandro was convinced that his wife had been unfaithful. Alejandro had disbelieved and rejected Jemima's pleas of innocence. So why did she still feel as though she had done something she shouldn't have done? Why was she shouldering the blame when she was the victim of Marco's lies and her husband's distrust?

In a sudden movement, Jemima scrambled out of bed and at the speed of light she pulled on her long silky aquamarine wrap before heading downstairs in search of Alejandro. Acting like the guilty party would win her no prizes and, recalling Alejandro's coldness earlier in the day just saying his brother's name, she knew that forgiveness wasn't even on the cards.

Alejandro wasn't at work in his study. He was outside on the terrace, his classic profile hard as iron as he leant up against a stone pillar and stared out at a midnight-blue night sky studded with twinkling stars. Jemima came to an uncertain halt in the doorway, the electric light framing her curling mane of silvery pale hair to give it rosy highlights while darkening the violet hue of her eyes and accentuating the soft vulnerable pink of her mouth.

'I thought you would be asleep by now,' Alejandro confessed, awarding her a single studied glance that was cool and unreadable.

'I'm not quite that thick-skinned,' she fenced back. 'I don't like being made to feel bad when I haven't done anything wrong.'

'Let's not go digging, *mi dulzura*.'

'Marco's pulled quite some number on you,' she condemned, her slight shoulders rigid with resentment, her spine ramrod straight. 'In choosing to believe your brother rather than your wife you've given him the power to torment you—'

Alejandro spun round in a fast fluid motion that took her by surprise. His lean, strong face was taut with suppressed emotion but his eyes were as golden, dazzling and aggressive in their fiery heat as the sun. '*Porque Demonios!* Nobody torments me,' he declared, his lean, powerful body poised like a panther's, about to leap on its prey.

'All right—*I'm* being tormented by this!' Jemima proclaimed, willing to bend the point and take the hit if it persuaded him to listen to her. She took a hurried step out into the warm night air. 'It's like a big chasm is opening up between us again.'

A sardonic ebony brow quirked. 'And you're *surprised*?'

Her cheeks flamed with embarrassment. She felt angry and bitter, hurt and fearful, all at one and the same time. It was not a good recipe for tact. Her temper on a razor edge, she resisted a needling, worrying urge to move closer to him because for the first time since she had returned to Spain she was afraid of rejection. 'Don't do this to us,' she muttered in urgent appeal.

His attention lingered on her, sliding from the full pout of her lips down to her slender, elegant throat and the dim white sloping valley of her breasts interrupted by the ribboned edge of her nightgown. 'Go back to bed before we say things that we won't be able to forget,' Alejandro urged with curt emphasis.

Jemima recognised the reserve that restrained him from matching her candour and feared the damage such diffidence might do. In her opinion, bottling things up only made problems fester. 'I'm not scared. I'm not running away. I *want* to be with you.'

'But possibly I don't want to be with you right now,' Alejandro murmured smooth as silk.

That admission hit Jemima like a brick and momentarily she felt stunned and reeled dizzily from that rebuff. He had once told her that when she was cornered she reacted like an alley cat, eager to scratch and bite. 'Only because you won't let yourself want me,' she challenged, padding nearer him on bare feet cooled by the worn granite tiling.

'You can be such a baby sometimes.' His beautiful obsidian gaze had a lethal gleam in the moonlight, the anger and rawness tamped down out of her sight, patently too private for her viewing. 'If I could put it all behind me and no longer think about it, I would have done so by now.'

In comparison, a cascade of happy images gleaned from recent weeks was flooding Jemima's thoughts. Everything she valued, not just happiness, was at risk and it terrified her. She cursed Marco and wished she had never befriended him and she hovered within reach of Alejandro, wanting to be needed, needing to be wanted if that was all she could have.

'Come to bed,' she whispered soft and low, despising herself for sinking low enough to play that card.

'I'm not up for that either tonight,' Alejandro asserted with chilling bite.

Talking to him in such a mood was like death by a thousand tiny cuts, Jemima reflected wildly. He was too controlled to shout at her. He wouldn't tell her what he was thinking, but then he didn't really need to, did he? Not when his derision could seep through the cracks to show on the surface and burn her like acid sprinkled on tender skin.

'Why did you ask me to give our marriage another chance if you were planning to behave like this?' Jemima slung at him accusingly.

'I never pretended I could give you a clean slate but I believe I've done reasonably well in the circumstances—'

'Well, I disagree!' Jemima shot at him furiously, temper clawing up through her with such speed and ferocity that the strength of her anger almost took *her* by surprise. 'In fact I think you are screwing our relationship up this time just the way you did last time.'

Alejandro viewed her with cold dark eyes that reflected the silvery moonlight. If she was an alley cat in a fight, he was the equivalent of a deadly rapier blade flashing without warning. '*I* screwed it up?' he traded very drily.

'When you are finally forced to accept that I *never* had an affair with your brother, who are you going to blame then?' Jemima demanded between gritted teeth. 'But at the rate you're going now, we won't last that long. You might not be forgiving, Alejandro, but neither am I and I'm beginning to think that I've wasted enough of my youth on a dead relationship—'

His stunning bone structure was now visible below his bronzed skin, his potent tension patent in his set jaw line and the stillness of his tall muscular body. 'It's not dead—'

'Right at this minute it feels like it's as dead as a dodo,' Jemima pronounced, spelling out that comparison in defiant disagreement. 'I shouldn't be wasting time here on you. I should be getting a divorce and looking for a man who *really* wants me…not some guy tearing us both apart over an affair that never happened!'

'I *really* want you,' Alejandro bit out in raw dissent. 'I won't agree to a divorce.'

'Can't live with me, can't live without me,' Jemima parried shakily, fighting to get a grip on her flailing emotions. 'But I *can* get by without you. I've proved it. I had a good life in Charlbury St Helen's…'

His well-shaped mouth curled into a sardonic smile. 'But not so good that you weren't prepared to walk away from all of it to come back to a life of luxury with me!'

Turning pale with rage at that taunt, Jemima trembled. 'I only came back here to try again for Alfie's benefit. Don't you dare try to make out that I'm some sort of gold-digger!'

Silence fell like a blanket and it seemed to use up all the available oxygen as Jemima waited impatiently for him to take back that final taunt. He stared steadily back at her as if she had got what she deserved in that exchange and, in a way, she supposed she had. Her refusal to embrace the role of the disgraced wife caught out in adultery lay between them, an obstacle neither of them could overcome. Alejandro was very proud, but he might have managed to come to terms with what he believed she had done had she enabled him to believe that she was truly sorry. In the absence of that development there was no natural way forward and both of them were stuck in their respective opposite corners.

Her small face stiff, Jemima threw him a look of angry reproach. 'I never wanted you for your money,' she told him heatedly. 'I may have got in a bit of a mess and spent more money than I should have done when we were first married, but it wasn't done out of greed and there was never any plan to rip you off.'

His brilliant gaze was intent but wary and locked to her every changing expression. 'I can believe that,' he said, surprising her with that declaration of faith.

'I am really sorry about the money—I was stupid,' Jemima admitted, warming to a topic that she could be honest about on at least one level. She had indeed been stupid: she had thrown away thousands and thousands of pounds and yet she still could not bring herself to tell him what she had done with it.

Alejandro took a jerky step forward. 'It was a case of bad timing. My business enterprises were over-extended. The winds of recession were howling around us and I was struggling to just hold onto what I had. It was the worst possible moment for you to go mad with money... but then I shouldn't have left you access to so much of it.'

Jemima was breathing rapidly and by the time he had finished speaking her lower lip had dropped fully away from the upper while she gaped at him in unconcealed astonishment. 'Are you saying that you had financial problems a couple of years ago when we were still living together?' she gasped in disbelief. 'But why didn't you tell me?'

Alejandro's handsome mouth compressed into a wry line. 'I didn't want to worry you...'

Her wide eyes prickled with a sudden hot rush of spontaneous tears. 'But I thought you were *so* rich,' she framed before she could think better of using that immature phraseology.

'I know. I knew you hadn't a clue there was anything to worry about,' Alejandro murmured ruefully. 'But the truth is that my father left so much money to my stepmother and Marco when he died that up until quite recently it was a struggle for me just to keep the estate afloat.'

Jemima was shaking her head slowly back and forth in a negative motion. She could not hide how shocked she was by what he had confessed. 'I had no idea. You really should have told me, Alejandro. In fact, not only did you not tell me there was a problem, you seemed to go out of your way to throw loads of money and expensive gifts at me,' she reminded him tautly. 'Why the heck did you do that?'

'You wanted the whole fairy tale along with the castle and I very much wanted you to have it as well,' Alejandro admitted with a wry twist of his mouth. 'How could I tell you that I was in danger of losing it all?'

'All the hours you were working, turning night into day…you were never at home,' she muttered unsteadily, fighting to hold the tears back with all her might. 'You were trying to keep your businesses afloat?'

'Yes, and the extra work did pay off in one regard. I secured new contracts and in the end the financial tide turned, but by then it was too late: I had lost my wife,' Alejandro intoned bleakly.

Her generous mouth wobbled at that reminder. She wanted to hug him, but at the same time she wanted to slap him really hard for keeping secrets from her. He had treated her like a fragile little girl who couldn't cope with the grown up stuff when, in actuality, she had never been that naïve even as a child. She was appalled to appreciate that he had undertaken such a struggle and worked such long thankless hours while she went out on endless shopping trips and went out at night clubbing with Marco.

'Alejandro…if you had told me the truth, shared the bad stuff with me instead of leaving me in ignorance, things would have been so very different,' Jemima breathed unevenly, tears rolling down her cheeks unchecked until she dashed a hand across her face in an embarrassed gesture and sniffed furiously. 'I would've understood. I would have made allowances.'

Alejandro braced a hand to her slender spine and pressed her back indoors where he handed her a tissue. 'I'm not sure anything would have been different. You were very young and naïve and you were already pregnant and unhappy and at the time I don't think you could have coped with any more stress.'

He was wrong, but she didn't argue with him because she was too choked up to do so. She knew that as much as anything else his fierce pride would have prevented him from telling her that he had financial problems. He was an old-fashioned guy and he had always seen it as solely his role to provide for her needs. He had loved to spoil her with unexpected gifts and treats, to give her the frills he knew she had never had before she met him. She could have cried her heart out in that instant for all she had truly wanted from him two years earlier were his precious time and attention, not his wealth or what it could buy her.

'I didn't expect you to be my superhero all the time,' Jemima told him awkwardly, her voice hoarse as she dabbed at her damp cheeks. 'If you'd confided in me, I would never have spent so much time with your brother. I felt neglected. I thought you regretted marrying me and you were bored and that that's why you never came home.'

'It never would have occurred to me that telling you I was on the brink of losing everything, including our home, might save my marriage,' Alejandro confided, his cynical doubt in that likelihood unconcealed.

'Well, that just goes to show how very little you know about me. I'm very loyal and I would have stuck by you through thick and thin!' Jemima claimed proudly.

'But in those days I think you had much more in

common with my fun-loving brother,' Alejandro murmured with a derisive edge to his dark deep drawl.

'I wasn't that shallow.' Although she was back in control of her emotions and composed again, Jemima's fingers still bit into the damp tissue clutched between her fingers. She had really, really loved him two years earlier and she wished he could at least accept that the love had been genuine and real, even if it hadn't proved strong enough to withstand the misfortunes that had engulfed them both. 'But you didn't give me the chance to be anything else.'

Casting a last lingering look at his breathtakingly handsome features from below damp feathery lashes, Jemima walked back up to bed without another word. Her mobile phone was flashing on the dressing table and she lifted it. She had missed one phone call and there were two text messages. One was from Beatriz, saying that she hoped that Jemima didn't mind her having given her brother her phone number. The second text and the missed call were from Marco and she jerked in shock when she realised that he had actually dared to get in touch with her again.

Must see you to talk. Urgent, ran his message.

Jemima deleted the text with stabbing fingers and tossed the phone down again. Marco had to be joking. In the current climate she was not prepared to take the risk of seeing him again even if she did have questions of her own to ask. My goodness, wouldn't Alejandro just love that? The last thing her marriage needed was more fuel for the same fire.

The door opened, startling her. She froze when she saw Alejandro and then she slid out of bed like an eel and sped over to him, wrapping her arms round his neck and letting her head fall back as he meshed one strong hand into the depths of her pale hair and kissed her breathless.

'I thought you wouldn't come,' she confided, heart thrumming like a plucked string on a violin, the full effect pulsing through her entire body along with her intense relief that he had not stayed away from her.

'*Dios mio!* Living apart won't help us. Been there, done that, *querida*,' he reminded her darkly. 'We might as well have been living in different houses while you were pregnant with Alfie. It made everything worse.'

Her generous mouth swollen from the onslaught of his, Jemima got back into bed. His arrival had already made her feel two hundred per cent happier. 'Well, that was your choice, not mine,' she traded cheekily.

His ebony brows pleated as he shed his suit. 'It wasn't anyone's choice, it was a necessity.'

'How was it a necessity?' she questioned once he had emerged from the bathroom and joined her in bed.

'Right from the start, Dr Santos was afraid you would miscarry. He was quite frank with me. You are very small and slightly built and it was obvious early on that what we thought was one baby was going to be big. I didn't stay happy that you were pregnant for very long,' Alejandro admitted heavily, his arm tightening round her to pull her closer. 'I felt hugely guilty for putting you at risk.'

'I wasn't at risk.'

'I felt that you were and with my own mother having died from complications in childbirth it was not a matter I could ever take lightly.'

Jemima mulled that over, registering that her obstetrician had been more honest with her husband than he had been with her. Or had he been? Her Spanish had been less fluent in those days and it was perfectly possible that she had misunderstood some of what he told her, picking up only the gist rather than the full meaning of his advice. That he had shared his apprehension with Alejandro, however, was news to her and that Alejandro had been seriously worried about her was also a surprise. Suddenly she frowned as she made another deduction.

'Are you saying that you stopped making love to me because Dr Santos warned you off?'

'Why else would I have stopped?' Alejandro growled soft and low in her ear, tugging her back into the heat of his long, hard body. Her nostrils flared on the husky scent of his skin and she quivered with awareness. 'I used another bedroom, not only because I was keeping late hours and didn't want to waken you but also because I didn't trust myself in the same bed with you any more.'

'You should've explained—I had no idea.'

'I was present when the doctor warned you that you would have to be very careful indeed if you wanted the pregnancy to go to term. You had already had some bleeding,' he reminded her grimly. 'I know I didn't discuss it with you but what was there to say? We didn't have a choice.'

She pressed her mouth in silent apology against a bare bronzed shoulder. Consternation had a strong grip on her. She was shaken by how badly she had misjudged his past behaviour. She had viewed everything through the distorting prism of her unhappiness and insecurity and two and two had seemed to make four but she had added up the facts incorrectly. Alejandro had not been bored with her. He had not deliberately neglected her either.

At a difficult time he had simply done the best that he could for the two of them, while her behaviour had only added to their problems. That acknowledgement shamed her and made her appreciate just how much she had grown up since then.

'Let's make an agreement,' Alejandro breathed in a measured undertone above her head. 'You stay away from Marco. You don't speak to him, you don't see him. That will keep the peace.'

Jemima had stiffened, taken aback by that proposition coming at her out of the blue. She drew in a quivering breath. 'All right…if that's what you want.'

'That's how it *has* to be,' Alejandro countered in a tone of finality.

'I'm not arguing. I couldn't care less. It's not a problem,' she muttered in a small voice.

The tension in his big powerful frame eased and he smoothed a soothing hand over her hair. 'Go to sleep,' he intoned huskily. 'If you don't, you'll be too tired to join me for breakfast in the morning. I'm leaving early for a board meeting in Seville.'

That he was already planning breakfast in her company made her smile. She was remembering the hot sexual passion of the afternoon in the hotel room, but lying in his arms there in their own bed felt so much more intimate and significant. Even after news that neither one of them had wanted to hear, they were still together. The agreement Alejandro had demanded warned her that she would be walking a knife edge if she defied him, but she had no such intention. Marco might be home, but she was not prepared to allow him to damage her marriage a second time.

The following morning, Alejandro left her enjoying

her coffee on the roof and Alfie went downstairs with Placida so that their son could watch his father's helicopter take off from the front lawn. Jemima was still sitting outside, lightly clad in a cotton sundress, when Beatriz came up to join her. Her sister-in-law looked strained.

'Was I wrong to give Marco your cell-phone number last night?' the brunette prompted anxiously. 'He was so eager for the chance to speak to you that when he pressed me, I didn't know what to do for best.'

'I'm afraid I don't want to speak to him,' Jemima admitted quietly.

'But if you and Marco talked and then you talked to Alejandro, maybe all this bad feeling could be put away,' Beatriz suggested with unconcealed hope. 'The way things are now is very awkward for all of us and it's only going to get more difficult once word gets out that Marco is home again. Our relatives and neighbours will soon start including him in their invitations. Nobody outside these walls is aware that my brothers are at odds with each other—'

'How can that be? I assumed your stepmother would have told tales about me everywhere after I left Spain to go home,' Jemima admitted with an expressive shudder.

'Not when she believed her son might have been involved with you. Doña Hortencia is very proud of the family name and her goal was to protect Marco's reputation, rather than yours,' Beatriz told her ruefully. 'She's hoping that now he's home he'll find a girl to marry.'

Jemima stiffened at that comment. 'Your stepmother might have quite a long wait.'

Was that an answering glint of amusement in her

sister-in-law's dark eyes? It was there and then it was gone and Jemima wondered if she had imagined it. Not for the first time Jemima wondered just how much Beatriz might know about her younger brother's life. The habit of silence, however, kept her quiet for she could not credit that Beatriz might know what Alejandro did not even appear to suspect. It was never easy to tell with Beatriz, though, because the brunette was always very discreet and cautious even with her own family. Beatriz liked to mind her own business and steer clear of trouble, but lately it had come to light that she could also stand up for herself when she had to. She had helped her stepmother move into her very comfortable house on the estate and had withstood the storm of being accused of ingratitude and selfishness when she'd revealed that she was planning to stay on below her brother's roof. Jemima valued the other woman's friendship and wished that she could have confided in her. She missed Flora's company and chatter, she acknowledged ruefully, and wondered if her friend would be able to come out to Spain for a visit any time soon.

The following week, Jemima spent some time reorganising rooms with the housekeeper, Maria. She was keeping busy because Alejandro had spent several days working in Seville. A room was being set up for use as a smaller, cosier dining room in place of the huge banqueting space and even vaster pieces of antique furniture, which Doña Hortencia had considered necessary to her dignity. Jemima wondered if she should have discussed the change with Alejandro first, and then wrinkled her nose and decided to follow her own preferences. When she mentioned anything to do with the interior workings of the household Alejandro generally looked blank and hastened to disclaim either interest or authority. When Maria spoke to someone behind her, she was fixing some flowers for the table in an effort to give the room a touch of the feudal magnificence that the Vasquez family pretty much took for granted in their daily life.

'Jemima...'

Violet eyes wide, Jemima flipped round and focused on the tall broad-shouldered male in the doorway. She paled. With his coal black curls he was a very good-looking, younger version of his big brother, although he was not so tall nor so powerfully built. He was also so well dressed that he closely resembled a model who had stepped out of a glossy magazine.

'Marco?' she whispered in dismay. 'I didn't want to see you.'

'That's not very friendly, is it?' Marco said in reproach. 'We are family, after all.'

CHAPTER NINE

JEMIMA reached a sudden decision and told Maria that she would finish the room on her own. As the house-keeper departed Jemima closed the door behind her, leant back against it and focused on Marco.

'I can't believe you've got the nerve to come any-where near me,' she admitted, her bright eyes sparkling with angry hostility.

Marco frowned. 'I don't understand why you are so angry with me.'

Registering that Alejandro's brother had decided to act as if he were ignorant of what he had done, Jemima tensed up like a racehorse at the start line. 'You're not stupid. You know very well why I'm angry. How *could* you allow Alejandro to believe that we had had an affair?'

'You had already left the country. Your marriage was over. What difference did it make to you what he thought?' he questioned, treating her to a level look that implied that he still had no real grasp of what the problem was.

'Doesn't it make a difference to you? It *should* do. Don't you have any affection for your brother that you could let him believe such a thing of us both?' Jemima slung back at him furiously.

Marco breathed in deep. 'All right, I'll try to be honest with you. I didn't really care what anyone thought if it gave me a good reason to leave home and move to New York. Dario and I needed the privacy to lead our own lives. As I honestly believed that you and Alejandro were all washed up as a couple, I didn't think it mattered.'

'You're not that innocent,' Jemima countered between compressed lips, any patience she had left fast shredding in the face of Marco's brazen refusal to express an ounce of regret, particularly when he was tossing his own relationship in her teeth and pointing out that he had wanted and needed it to prosper. 'You could have gone to New York with Dario and without hurting and humiliating your brother with that filthy lie!'

His smooth brow furrowed. 'I didn't actually tell any lies,' he retorted with an infuriating air of condescension. 'I didn't have to. Alejandro was convinced that you and I had had an affair and I didn't deny it. As far as I was concerned, if he wanted to believe something so ridiculous, that was his business and nothing to do with me—'

'It had everything to do with you!' Jemima yelled back at him. 'You didn't care who got hurt. You used our supposed relationship as an excuse—'

'Your marriage was over,' Marco reminded her afresh. 'I didn't know you were still pregnant—'

'I didn't know either at the time I left Spain,' Jemima conceded unwillingly.

'Naturally if I had known there was going to be a child it would have made a difference to what I allowed my brother to believe,' Marco argued. 'But I had no idea.'

'Well, you know now and I'm back with Alejandro

and we're trying to make a go of our marriage again,' Jemima pointed out. 'Only that's not very easy when he still thinks that I slept with you...'

'My brother has always had an easy ride through life. Everything always fell perfectly into place for him, at school, in business, with women,' Marco enumerated with a bitter resentment that he could not hide. 'A little bit of suffering over you and his marriage probably did wonders for his character.'

At that unfeeling crack, Jemima had to struggle to hang onto her temper because she had already decided that telling Marco exactly what she thought of him would be a counterproductive rather than positive act when she needed him to redress the wrong that he had done. Now she marvelled that she had not previously appreciated just how much Marco envied his brother's success in every field. Had she known what was really in Marco's heart she would never have made him her confidant or trusted him as much as she had. Just how much had his unrelenting negativity about her marriage influenced her when it came to making the decision to leave her husband? She did not want to think about that.

'You *have* to tell Alejandro the truth.'

Marco shook his handsome head, his eyes guarded. 'No can do.'

'Well, that's your decision,' Jemima said tightly in the tense silence, her teeth gritting on an urge to be a good deal more aggressive. 'But you can't expect me to stay quiet. If you won't tell Alejandro the truth, I *will*.'

Apprehension now tightening his boyish features, Marco strode forward. 'But you promised to keep my secret.'

Jemima lifted her chin, the anger in her clear gaze an open challenge. 'I didn't know then how much damage keeping your secret was likely to do to my marriage. Surely you can be honest now with your family?' she said forcefully. 'It may not be what they want for you, or expect, but families have got over worse revelations.'

'As far as my mother is concerned, there could be no *worse* revelation than the news that the love of my life is a boy and not a girl,' Marco declared in scornful disagreement. 'Have you ever heard her talking about gay people?'

Jemima grimaced and nodded confirmation. 'She is prejudiced but that could well change if you talked to her and gave her the chance to understand who you really are.'

'You've got to be joking!' Marco snapped back at her, angry colour edging his cheekbones. 'She'd throw me out of the house and cut off my allowance!'

Jemima's brows knitted and she studied him with narrowed eyes. 'I wasn't aware that you received an allowance from your mother.'

Marco released his breath in a weary groan. 'Do you really think that I could afford to live as comfortably as I do on an employee's salary?'

Stepping away from the door, Jemima stiffened. 'Your financial arrangements are none of my business, Marco. Whether you tell your mother or not is nothing to do with me either. But Alejandro is my business and I *do* expect you to tell him that you're gay so that he, at least, can appreciate that we did not have an affair.'

Marco sent her a furious look of umbrage. 'I'm certainly not telling Alejandro. He sacked the only gay man on his staff—did he tell you that?'

'Yes, but I believe the guy in question was also a bully and had had several warnings about the way he'd treated other staff before he was fired. I have never seen or heard Alejandro do or say anything which would lead me to believe that he has homophobic views. He doesn't share your mother's religious outlook on the issue either,' Jemima reasoned levelly. 'I'm not asking you to do this, Marco, I'm telling you that if you don't tell your brother, I will do it for you. I don't have to keep your secret when it's threatening to wreck my happiness and my child's.'

'You're blackmailing me,' Marco accused her angrily.

'I don't owe you any explanations or apologies after what you did to Alejandro,' Jemima contended, lifting her chin in challenge. 'I don't owe you anything.'

Registering that she was serious and not about to back down, Marco lost his temper. Throwing her a furious look of hostility, he swore at her. Then he yanked open the door with an impatient hand, stalked past the astonished housekeeper in the hall and straight back out of the castle. Jemima breathed in deep and slow and returned to the flower arrangement she had been doing. Beatriz joined her and admired the room, remarking that its more comfortable proportions would be a great deal warmer and more pleasant during the cooler months of the year when the fires were lit. For just a few minutes in the other woman's soothing company, it seemed to Jemima that the raw, distressing little scene with Marco had only taken place within her own imagination.

She couldn't help but think back to their former friendship. She had also just learned something from Marco that shed a rather different light on the past. Marco was financially dependent on his mother's continuing goodwill and, if Doña Hortencia's past pronouncements were anything to go by, it was very possible that Marco's admission that he was gay would lead to the kind of ructions that might well hit him hard in the pocket. Was that why Marco had always gone to such lengths to conceal his sexuality? Had money always been the primary reason for his silence on that issue? It occurred to Jemima that she had once been incredibly naïve and trusting when it came to Marco.

Retaining her brother-in-law's friendship, she acknowledged sadly, had come at a high cost, for she had been forced to conceal more and more from her husband. Marco had used her as an alibi and a front when he went places where he preferred not to be seen without female company. His Italian boyfriend, Dario, had often accompanied them on those nights out. What had happened to the open and honest nature that she had once prided herself on having? Almost from the start of her marriage she had begun to keep secrets from Alejandro.

That thought made her heart sink and her mind return to a place she didn't want to revisit. The past was best left untouched, she reckoned uneasily. There would be no advantage to digging everything up. Alejandro would be grateful for all of five minutes when she told him the truth of what she had done with the large sums of money that she had taken from their joint account over two years earlier. But five minutes after that he would wish she had kept quiet and he would see her in yet another unflattering light. Once again she would be shown up as his less than perfect match. She didn't think their marriage could withstand a second blow of that type.

'Marco can be very volatile,' his sister, Beatriz,

remarked gingerly, her attention locked to Jemima's troubled and expressive face.

'Yes,' Jemima agreed.

'But if you ignore his moods, I've found that he soon gets over them,' Beatriz added comfortably. 'Doña Hortencia indulged him too much when he was a child.'

The housekeeper came to the door to pass on a message from Alejandro. He had phoned to say that he would be spending the night at the family apartment in Seville. Jemima's slim shoulders sagged. Only when she learned that he wasn't coming back did she realise how much she had been looking forward to seeing him that evening. In addition she was a little hurt that he had not thought to speak to her personally about his change of plan.

'Jemima…go to Seville and be with my brother,' Beatriz urged, causing Jemima's violet eyes to fly to her in shock. 'You want to be with Alejandro and why shouldn't you be? I'll ensure that Alfie has his bath and his bedtime story. In fact if you wouldn't mind I'm planning to visit my friend, Serafina, this afternoon and I'd like to take Alfie with me. Serafina has a toddler as well.'

All concerns laid to rest by Beatriz's willingness to entertain her nephew, Jemima went upstairs to change. She was delighted by the idea of surprising Alejandro, for she had never done anything like that before, indeed had always shrunk from putting her feelings for him on the line, but the connection they had formed since her return to Spain really did feel much deeper and stronger. There was nothing wrong with being confident and optimistic, she told herself urgently. Once Marco did what he had to do the dark shadow that her brother-in-law had cast over her marriage would soon disappear.

She was in her bedroom when the phone call came. Engaged in checking her reflection in a raspberry-coloured dress with a draped neckline that clung to the curve of her breasts, outlined her tiny waist and bared a good deal of her legs, she snatched up the receiver by the bed to answer it.

'Jem…is that you?' a rough-edged male voice demanded. 'The woman said she'd put me straight through to you.'

Jemima froze, the animated colour in her face fading fast to leave her white as milk. Her heart sank to the soles of her feet and she almost tottered back against the bed for support on legs that felt too woolly to keep her standing upright. She had hoped never, ever to hear that voice again but fate, it seemed, was too cruel to grant her that escape from the memory of past connections and mistakes. Too late did she remember the phone calls from the unnamed male that Maria had mentioned that she had missed.

'How did you know where to find me?' she asked tautly.

'Your cousin, Ellie, saw a picture of you in a magazine and showed it to me. My little Jem in an evening dress mixing with all the toffs like she's one of them!' the older man jeered. 'So you went back to live with that high and mighty Spanish count of yours and you never even got in touch to tell me.'

'Why would I have?' Jemima asked her father sickly.

'The magazine mentioned that you have a kiddy as well now—my grandson and I've not even seen him,'

Stephen Grey complained. 'Maybe I should pay you a visit. If I was to come out of the woodwork now and embarrass you, you'd have a lot to lose, Jem.'

'I haven't got any money…I'm not giving you anything,' Jemima protested feverishly. 'You can't threaten me any more. Just leave me alone!'

Without waiting for a response, Jemima cut off the call and stood there clutching the receiver so hard in her hand that it hurt her fingers. She wouldn't let it start up again. She wouldn't be a pushover this time around. She would stand up for herself and refuse to be alarmed and intimidated by his threats. But in the back of her mind she was already wondering how much of the money in her bank account it would take to keep her father quiet.

He was an evil, frightening man, who had abused both his wife and his daughter with his nasty tongue and his brutal fists, finally throwing Jemima out onto the street as a teenager and washing his hands of responsibility for her. She had made her own way in life no thanks to Stephen Grey. He had no right to demand money from her, no right to terrorize her. He would phone back, she *knew* he would phone back, or worse… come and pay her a visit as he had once before. She had paid him to keep his distance and keep his mouth shut two years ago and his hopes would be riding high that she would crumble and make the same mistake again.

And she was in this position all because early on in her relationship with Alejandro she had told a little white lie that had seemed harmless, she thought in anguish. In fact at the time it had felt like simple common sense to conceal the ugly truth. Conscious that Alejandro came from a much more privileged and respectable background than she did, she had seen no reason to trail out all the dirty washing that accompanied her own more humble beginnings. Indeed she had cringed from the prospect of telling Alejandro that her father had been imprisoned repeatedly, never mind broaching the reality that he'd also regularly beaten up her mother. She had lived a sad, grubby life as a child with a mother who drank herself into a stupor daily to escape the world and the husband she couldn't cope with.

In Seville, Jemima parked below the large office building that housed Alejandro's headquarters. When she arrived on the top floor she learned that he was in a meeting and thought that perhaps it had been a bad idea to spring a surprise on him when he was clearly so busy. She was just getting comfortable in Reception when two of Alejandro's executives passed by and, recognising her, stopped to chat.

A very profitable contract renegotiated and agreed, Alejandro saw his business colleagues and their lawyers off the premises before he discovered his wife surrounded by a little ring of admiring men in Reception. She was like a small but very powerful magnet, he conceded bleakly, watching her violet eyes sparkle with natural enticement as she laughed. Her jacket was hanging open, her slender but curvy little body on display. His handsome mouth compressed into a hard, ruthless line.

Jemima's gaze fell on Alejandro and she scrambled upright with a sunny smile to greet him. He looked outrageously handsome although even at a glance she recognised his leashed tension and assumed he was tired after a stressful day. 'Are you too busy for me?' she asked.

'I doubt if there is a man in the building who would

be too busy for you, *querida*,' he murmured, nodding as his executives acknowledged him and went on about their business. 'You look irresistible in that dress.'

But Jemima noticed that his brilliant answering smile didn't reach the cool darkness of his eyes and an odd little stab of alarm ran through her. As he guided her towards the lift with a firm hand at her spine that made her nerve-endings tingle she shot a glance at his hard bronzed profile. The dense screen of his black lashes cloaked his gaze even as an electrifying surge of awareness shimmied through her slender length. Within a heartbeat she was recalling the way his lean, powerful body had shuddered over hers in release around dawn and the all-consuming love that had overwhelmed her in his arms. She had never been a morning person but Alejandro had changed that. There was something intensely sexy about waking up next to his hot, hungry body. The merest touch made her ready for him and the reflection plunged her into a cascade of erotic imagery. By the time she emerged from that colourful daydream she was trembling and conscious that he had yet to break the heavy silence.

'Were you finished for the day?' she asked anxiously then. 'I mean, I didn't intend to just show up and force your hand.'

The lift doors whirred back to reveal the basement car park. 'I was ready to leave. Are you parked here?'

'Yes.'

'What brought you to Seville?' Alejandro enquired as his driver pulled in to pick them up a few yards from the lift.

Jemima went pink. 'You…I wanted to see you.'

Alejandro lifted a sardonic dark brow.

'Yes, I *did*!' Jemima proclaimed in the face of that disbelief.

'*Dios mio*—is it possible that you have something to tell me?' Alejandro enquired silkily.

Aware of the undertones of tension pulling at her, Jemima shifted uneasily and wondered why he was asking her that. 'No—what would I have to tell you?'

'Only you can answer that question,' Alejandro breathed icily.

Jemima shot him an enervated look and decided that while he always went for subtle she was more at home with being blunt. 'I'm no good at trick questions. Just tell me what's wrong.'

His lean dark features were taut, his eyes shielded. He said nothing. In the humming quiet, she stared out of the window at the crowded streets and waited in vain for his response.

'Well, this will certainly teach me a lesson. Don't go surprising you at the office…you're keeping such a distance from me I feel like Typhoid Mary!' she declared in flippant continuance, struggling to hide her hurt and mortification at the chilly welcome she had so far received from him.

'Exactly what did you expect from me?' Alejandro shot at her with dark eyes that flashed as golden as the heart of a fire.

As her bewilderment increased the limo came to a halt. They would walk the remaining distance through the pedestrian zone in the oldest part of Seville. The Vasquez apartment was in a gracious old building that had considerable character.

The anger that Alejandro could no longer hide was like a blast of heat on her unprotected skin. His driver opened the car door and they climbed out to walk down narrow streets past tall eighteenth-century houses and finally through a familiar flower-filled courtyard. By then her heart was beating as fast and loud as a jungle drum and a sheen of nervous perspiration had dampened her skin. They walked through tall gates and across the cobblestones towards an elegant building. She felt sick with apprehension.

'Why are you angry with me?' she prompted finally.

'Because you're a liar and I can't stay married to a woman I can't trust out of my sight!'

That thunderous aside punched through Jemima's defences like a hard physical blow. As she stepped into the old-fashioned lift fashioned of ornate wrought-iron folding gates she was in shock. She was a liar and he couldn't trust her? All of a sudden he was threatening to end their marriage? She could think of only one possible explanation for his behaviour.

Entering the cool, spacious apartment that spanned the equivalent of two buildings, Jemima stole an enervated glance at her tall, well-built husband and said abruptly, 'You know I've seen Marco, don't you? How?'

'When I phoned to speak to you, Maria mentioned that you were with him.'

Alejandro strode on into the airy drawing room where the shadows cast by the palm tree in the front courtyard were dancing in flickering spears of ghostly foliage across the pale walls. Once again the décor was new to her, the old darker, richer colours banished and replaced by shades that were light and new. The silence dragged horribly.

'Marco just came up to the castle to speak to me,'

Jemima told him jerkily, giving way first to the dreadful tension. 'Probably because he texted me and called last night and I didn't respond in any way.'

Alejandro rested unimpressed eyes on her, his wide sensual mouth taking on a contemptuous twist. 'And you didn't mention that fact to me, either.'

'Be fair,' Jemima urged in desperation. 'I didn't want a stupid text message and a missed call from Marco to cause more trouble between us.'

Alejandro turned blistering dark golden eyes on her. His fabulous bone structure was set in hard lines of restraint. 'Without trust I can't live with you,' he breathed with a suppressed savagery that raised gooseflesh on her exposed skin. 'How could it be otherwise? I believed that we were getting somewhere and then today I learned that you were with Marco, in *spite* of your promise to me.'

Jemima was trembling, nausea stirring in the pit of her stomach. She had never felt as alone or scared since childhood as she did at that moment. She could feel his strength, his force of will and his immovable resolve. If he decided that walking away from her was the right thing to do, he would do it, no matter what the cost. Unhappily for her she had promised not to see Marco and she had broken her promise. How could she defend herself from that charge?

It was not the moment, she sensed, to tell him that he was being unreasonable, and that, for as long as Marco was a family member with automatic access to their home, avoiding the younger man would be a challenge. Alejandro was not in a cool, rational state of mind, she conceded inwardly. Indeed he was containing so many powerful emotions that he radiated glowing energy. But she could feel the distance in him, the wall he was already erecting between them. She had wounded him and he had taken a mental step back from her and their marriage. She was so appalled by the awareness that he was talking about a divorce that she could barely think straight. She could not bear to have got Alejandro back, to have tasted that happiness and then lose it and him again; it would be too cruel to bear.

Too late she saw where she had gone wrong. She had seriously underestimated the damage being done by Alejandro's conviction that she had been unfaithful. And she had made that cardinal error because she had known that she was innocent and had loftily dismissed the likely fallout from his destructive belief that she was not to be trusted. But she could also be a fast learner. When she feared losing Alejandro, no other loyalty had the power to hold her and she broke the silence in haste.

'There's never been anything between your brother and me and he will be speaking to you about that by the end of the week,' Jemima told Alejandro in a feverish rush, too worked up to stop and plan what she had to say before she spoke.

Alejandro was frowning at her. 'What are you talking about?'

'Marco informed me that he never actually told you that we had had an affair—he just didn't deny your accusation. But, by the start of the weekend, you'll know the truth because either he or I will tell you why there was never any possibility of an affair…'

'*Porque demonios!*' Alejandro exclaimed in frustration at that tangled explanation. 'Stop talking to me in riddles!'

'I gave my word to Marco that I would let him talk to you before I did.'

Outrage flared in Alejandro's brooding scrutiny. 'If there is something that I should know, I demand that you tell me now!'

The silence closed round them, thick and heavy as treacle.

'Marco is gay.' Jemima almost whispered the words, conscious of the pledge she had given and even while she refused to be bound by it she felt the bite of guilt and regret all the same. 'So there was never any question of anything intimate between us.'

Alejandro studied her in irate consternation. 'Are you trying to come up with a good cover story now? That's a despicable lie to tell me about my brother.'

'I appreciate that what I've just told you may come as a shock to you, but I'm not lying or trying to come up with a story,' Jemima protested fiercely.

'My brother has been dating…very extensively…since he was sixteen years old. I think we would know by now if he were gay,' Alejandro proclaimed very drily, his lean, strong face hard with denial.

'Marco has done everything possible to hide his true nature and he was at university before he reached the conclusion that he was gay. The girlfriends were just part of the pretence he put up. Didn't you ever wonder why he never hung onto any of them for longer than a couple of weeks?'

'Not many young men in his age group want a serious relationship.'

An uncertain laugh fell from Jemima's lips. 'I'm not getting anywhere with you, am I? You just don't believe me but I am telling you the truth. Marco didn't want anyone to know, not you and particularly not his mother. I know Doña Hortencia's outlook and Marco was afraid she would cut off the allowance she gives him.'

'As there is no question of my brother being gay, we will not discuss the matter further,' Alejandro pronounced with derision, his sensual mouth curling with disdain. 'But I would not have believed that even you would sink as low as to tell such lies.'

Having paled, Jemima took another tack in the hope of convincing him. 'From what I can understand Marco is still with Dario Ortini,' she remarked gingerly.

'What has that to do with anything? They were students together. They're old friends.'

'*No*, they are much more than that to each other.' Jemima shook her head slowly, her pale cloud of hair shifting round her strained face as she voiced that confident assurance. 'They're a couple, Alejandro. And pretty much inseparable. Didn't you think it strange that Dario went to New York as well?'

Alejandro parted his lips as if he was going to speak again to argue with her, and then suddenly he frowned and slowly closed his mouth again. She could literally see him thinking over what she had told him, making the connections, and while the uneasy silence stretched she watched him travel gradually from a state of incomprehension and angry disbelief to one of troubled and stunned acceptance.

'I can hardly believe it,' Alejandro muttered. 'Dario, now, he is less of a surprise. But their continuing friendship does stretch credulity too far.'

Jemima studied Alejandro fixedly, recognising that he was still fighting his astonishment.

'Evidently my brother has been leading a double life

for years,' he intoned between compressed lips. '*Dios mio*. Why couldn't he just tell me? Did he believe I would think less of him? It doesn't matter a damn to me—he is still my brother. But why the hell did Marco allow me to go on believing that you and he had had an affair?'

Jemima brushed her hair off her damp brow with an impatient hand. 'He's jealous of you, well, *very* jealous of everything you've achieved in life,' she divulged reluctantly.

'It is true that he has always been very competitive with me,' Alejandro acknowledged.

'I don't know how he could let you go on believing there had been an affair, but that's something you need to discuss with him rather than me.'

'Right now, what I need is a strong drink,' Alejandro admitted in a raw undertone, striding over to the drinks cabinet and asking her what she would like.

She closed a damp palm round the moisture-beaded tumbler he handed to her and pressed the glass against the overheated skin below her collarbone, all the while watching Alejandro, noticing how pale he was beneath his bronzed complexion and how prominent his hard bone structure seemed. His hands weren't quite steady either: he was really uptight.

'Are you all right?' she whispered worriedly.

'No,' he admitted flatly. 'I'm shattered, absolutely bloody shattered. My brother is gay and I never even suspected the fact.'

'That was how Marco wanted it. He didn't want his family to know.'

'My stepmother will throw a fit.' Alejandro scored long brown fingers through his luxuriant black hair, tousling it into disorder and turning his handsome head to study Jemima again with intense dark eyes. 'But, right at this moment, it is more important that I concentrate on what I've done to you and our marriage. I condemned you, misjudged you, refused to accept your word.'

Jemima gave an awkward shrug. 'I'm just grateful that you finally know and accept the truth. I can understand that when Marco didn't deny the affair you found it hard to believe that nothing had ever happened between us.'

'He used you to get at me. I should have had more faith in you.' Alejandro drained his glass and set it down in a hasty movement. 'Let's go out to eat.'

The abrupt change of mood and focus took her aback but it was very much Alejandro's way to reclaim his space and self-discipline. She had broken through his reserve with her revelation and he wanted the breathing space to put all those messy emotions back again where she couldn't see them. He continually frustrated her with his refusal to share what he thought and felt, she thought ruefully. She wanted to throw herself in his arms and tell him that she loved him enough to forgive him, but she sensed that that would not be a comfort. Alejandro was very proud. He had such high standards and, unhappily for him, he had just failed those standards. He had to come to terms with that and deal with it in his own way.

They dined only a few streets away in a tiny restaurant where the food melted in her mouth to be washed down by the finest wine. Alejandro had reinstated his iron self-control, for not a single reference to his brother passed his lips. In the candlelight she reached for his hand once and he gripped her fingers so tightly he almost crushed them.

'Don't say anything,' he urged in a roughened growl that was as much a plea as a command. 'I would rather have your anger than your pity, *tesora mia*.'

Sensing that a change of subject would be timely Jemima asked him when he had had the apartment redecorated.

'Soon after you left Spain, I still imagined you were waiting for me every time I walked through the door. I didn't like it,' he confessed, his dark, deep accented drawl as clipped as if he were talking business.

'And when you went into our bedroom at the castle?'

'The same.' He shrugged a broad shoulder in dismissal, subject closed.

He was more sensitive than she had ever appreciated, she conceded, and it was a discovery that troubled her more than it pleased her, for it made her think about the trauma he must have suffered when he'd believed she had betrayed him in his brother's arms. He hadn't needed to love her to be hurt. Marco had struck at the very roots of his sibling's pride and possessiveness, and his strong and protective family instincts, and it had been a devastating blow on all fronts.

Later, she slid naked and alone between the white linen sheets of the king-sized bed in the master bedroom. Alejandro had said he had work to catch up on before morning when they were to fly back home. Work, or a preference for his own company? She tossed and turned, wanting to be with him, refusing out of pride to make that move. He wasn't weak; why should she be? Giving into love was a weakness when it was for a man who did not love her back and who would despise any attempt to offer him reassurance. Eventually she fell into an uneasy doze, waking again with a jerk. She put on the light to check her watch and the empty bed. It was three in the morning and her resistance to natural promptings was at its lowest ebb. She thrust back the sheet and padded off in search of her missing husband.

And when she did, she discovered that Alejandro still had the power to surprise her...

CHAPTER TEN

JEMIMA knew drunk when she saw it. An awareness of the signs was etched deep in her psyche after a childhood in which a man's stumbling steps or a mother's shrill slurred complaints could make her turn cold with fear or insecurity. And with them went an out-of-control sensation that Jemima herself did not like, which was why she never, ever drank and why she had been happy to marry a man of abstemious habits.

But undeniably and disturbingly, Alejandro was the worse for wear because of alcohol. He was in the lounge, bathed only in moonlight as the curtains were still open wide. He was barefoot, his jeans unbuttoned at his narrow waist and his white shirt hung open on his bronzed muscular chest. But as he lurched upright to acknowledge her entrance he swayed and almost lost his footing. He steadied himself with a timely hand on a carved lamp table. His ebony hair was dishevelled, his stubborn jaw line rough with stubble and his midnight-dark eyes had a wild glitter unfamiliar to her.

'Alejandro?' Her violet eyes were full of concern; it was a question as much as a greeting.

She watched him struggle to focus and regroup. 'I can't talk to you right now—'

'You're going to talk to me whether you want to or not. Anything is better than you sitting drinking alone!' Jemima pronounced, a small hand pouncing on the bottle of spirits on the coffee table before he could reach for it again.

For a split second, outrage flashed over his lean dark features because he had been prevented from doing what he wanted to do. Then he froze as if he was registering that he had been caught in a less than presentable state and wasn't quite sure how to handle that exposure.

'You've been drinking and I want to know why,' Jemima spelt out.

With a visible effort, Alejandro squared his broad shoulders, muscles rippling across his flat, hard stomach as he sucked in a shuddering breath. 'Not now...'

Her violet eyes softened. 'I *need* to understand why,' she rephrased gently.

'Isn't that obvious? I got everything in our marriage wrong!' he launched at her with an explosive wrath that had finally escaped his containment. *'Everything!'*

Jemima sighed. 'It happens. You just have to live with it.'

'No sympathy?' A black brow lifted.

'You put me through hell. You don't deserve it,' she told him bluntly.

'You have the power to drive me mad with jealousy— you always did,' he confided harshly, his lean bronzed profile bleak. 'I saw you with another man once and I never forgot the way it made me feel.'

Jemima's brow had pleated. 'When?' she cut in.

'Long before we were married. That time you decided that if I was seeing other women you would see another man,' he specified.

Undaunted by the reminder, Jemima tilted her chin. 'That was fair enough,' she commented.

'You were in the street, smiling at him the same way you smiled at me and he was holding your hand,' Alejandro recalled, his dark eyes brooding with remembered hostility and recoil. 'I couldn't stand it. There is nothing I wouldn't have done to get him out of your life! But that predilection for jealousy stayed with me. It's in my nature.'

She remembered how fast their relationship had become exclusive once Alejandro had realised that the agreement had to cut both ways. But it was news to her that his demon jealousy had continued to dog him.

In the simmering silence, Alejandro clenched his hands into powerful fists. He sent her a burning look of condemnation from below the fringe of his lush black lashes. 'If you want honesty, I'll give it to you. I hated you spending so much time with my brother three years ago. I tried very hard to be reasonable about it. I knew I was working too many hours. I knew you were bored and unhappy, but you and Marco got on too well. You seemed so close. Of course it bothered me at a time when our marriage was under strain. I thought I was losing you. Naturally I began to believe that you had more than a platonic friendship going with my brother.'

'Even though I was pregnant with Alfie and was as sick as a dog for weeks on end?' Jemima pressed, keen to bring him to an awareness of how far-fetched his fears had been in the circumstances.

'Your friendship with Marco started months before that. He was always seeking you out, phoning you, sharing secret jokes with you…'

'I suppose we were too close for comfort. He told

me his big secret that he was gay and it made me feel privileged,' she muttered ruefully. 'I just didn't realise that you could be jealous of me because you never let me see it.'

'I was too proud to show you my Achilles' heel. But the jealousy tortured me and twisted the way I saw everything,' he revealed in a roughened admission. 'I thought you were taunting me with your preference for Marco's company.'

Jemima swallowed and then spoke up even though she didn't want to speak up on that angle. 'There was an element of that in my attitude. I so wanted your attention. I thought that if you saw how much Marco liked being with me it might make you want to spend more time with me,' she confessed unhappily. 'I didn't know that you were working so hard because you were trying to keep your businesses afloat. I thought you were bored with me.'

'I felt many things when we were first married but boredom never featured for even five minutes,' Alejandro revealed with a look of sardonic amusement marking his lean, darkly handsome features.

In the moonlight, which silvered his bronzed skin and accentuated the angles and hollows of his sculptured face, his sheer masculine beauty took her breath away. It crossed her mind that she now loved him much more deeply than she had when she first married him. She saw the man and his flaws. He wasn't perfect but it didn't matter because neither was she. But all that truly mattered to her just then was that he had never stopped wanting her before or after their marriage. Jealousy, assuming he could keep it within bounds, well, she could live with it by understanding that all that deep dark emotion of his had to occasionally find the wrong outlet.

'Why were you drinking?' she asked him worriedly.

Alejandro released a bleak laugh that was like a cold hand trailing down her spine. He settled haunted dark eyes on her, his tension unrelieved by their discussion. 'I let you down. I let you down in every way that mattered. You were my wife and, instead of supporting you and caring for you, I accused you of sleeping with my brother. Then I drove you away.'

'But now you know the truth.'

'And like many truths, it's not one I will enjoy living with.' Lean, powerful face grim, he yanked off his shirt in a physical move that startled her and strode past her, his steps even, his head high as though the very act of having had to talk to her had sobered him up. 'I need a shower.'

And Jemima went back to bed and lay awake waiting for him, but wherever he went to wash it wasn't in the en suite bathroom that adjoined the master bedroom. And wherever he slept it was not with her.

The next morning, however, it was business as usual for Alejandro. There was not a hint of the night's excesses visible in his crackling vitality and immaculately dressed appearance or, indeed, in his light and courteous conversation over breakfast. He'd made arrangements for the car she had driven to Seville to be returned to the estate and they left for the airfield and the short flight home. Alfie came running out into the garden to greet his parents and Alejandro snatched his son off his feet and hugged him close with an unashamed affection that touched Jemima's heart while making her crave the same treatment. Why were pride and perfection so important to Alejandro? Why could she accept his faults and live with them so much more easily than he could hers? She hadn't expected a perfect man and she hadn't got one. A more enlightened husband willing to accept that there was a learning curve in their marriage was the very best she could reasonably hope for. The difference between them was that she was already happy with the balance they had achieved now that he knew the truth about her supposed 'affair'.

It was the very next day that she received her second phone call from her father. She was with Alejandro when the call arrived and she excused herself to take it.

'It's normal for a man to expect his daughter to help him out,' Stephen Grey told her in a self-pitying whine. 'I'm not long out of prison, times are tough...'

'Have you tried to find work?' Jemima enquired flatly.

'It's not that easy.'

'You've never worked, never tried to keep yourself honestly. I'm not giving you any money this time.'

'How can you be so selfish? You're married to a very rich man. I've done my homework on him. You can afford to be generous—'

'I don't intend to spend the rest of my life being blackmailed by you. I've said no. You're out of luck. I'm not giving you a single euro of my husband's hard-earned cash. For a start, it's not mine to give,' Jemima asserted with cold clarity, and she replaced the phone receiver the instant she heard the warning rumble of her father's abusive response beginning.

She felt hot with shame when she recalled how she had first given way to her father's threats almost three years earlier, recklessly and fearfully handing over cash that she now knew Alejandro had not been able to afford just to keep the older man silent. Now she was calling Stephen Grey's bluff while dreading the prospect that he might go to the newspapers to reveal their relationship. The sleazy tale of her father's criminality and her unsavoury background and upbringing could only embarrass Alejandro and his family.

'Who was that on the phone?' Alejandro asked when she joined him and her son in the swimming pool, her slender body fetchingly clad in a ruffled apricot bikini.

'Oh, just someone from home.' Jemima struggled to telegraph casualness and lifted and dropped a thin shoulder while feeling the stiff discomfiture of virtually lying to him handicapping her pretence. 'Nobody important.'

It seemed to her that Alejandro's dark golden eyes rested on her a little longer than they need have done but, mercifully, he said nothing and went back to the task of teaching Alfie to swim. Very much a water baby, her son paddled over to her and giggled as he splashed her. The movement of the water was like cool silk lapping against Jemima's overheated skin. She rested back against the side and took in the sweeping view of the lush valley encircled by the snow-capped peaks. Her marriage had a horizon and a future again. She was not about to let go of that without a fight.

In the week that followed, Alejandro went out of his way to spend time with her and Alfie but, even though he returned to the marital bed, he didn't make love to her again. They dined out twice and on the second occasion he gave her a fabulous diamond ring just before they went out.

'What is this for?' she asked helplessly over dinner, watching the light flash blindingly on the glittering jewel and knowing that such magnificence must have cost at least two arms and a leg.

His ebony brows drew together, his dark golden eyes level. 'You're my wife. It's natural for me to want to give you gifts.'

'As long as it's not your guilty conscience talking,' Jemima cut in uncomfortably. 'You don't need to buy me, Alejandro. You already have me.'

'Do I? That's not something I would like to take for granted. You like pretty things,' he drawled softly. 'And I like giving them to you. I always did.'

Jemima turned a guilty pink. 'I had a fairly dismal childhood and I suppose I'm still making up for what I didn't get then.'

'You never talk about your childhood.'

Jemima tensed and shrugged, fixing a bright smile to her full mouth that felt hopelessly false. 'There's not much to talk about. We were always short of money and my parents didn't get on very well. It certainly wasn't a marriage made in heaven.'

'I seem to recall you telling me that your mother died in a car crash.'

'Yes. It was a sad time,' she said quickly, striving to steer him away from further discussion in that line because she did not want to be forced to tell him any more untruths. Somehow lies told in the past when they had seemed to have no relevance bothered her less than the prospect of having to tell more in the present.

After a stressful week, her nerves were still on a cliff edge of doubt, fear and uncertainty with regard to the future. Her father had phoned twice more, one call arriving when she was out and the second proving to be more or less a repeat of the first one she had received, in which he bemoaned his financial state, urged her to be generous and threatened to come and visit her in Spain. The last time Stephen Grey had insisted on being paid in untraceable cash, and although Jemima had sworn she would not pay blackmail money again, she knew to the last pound sterling how much money she had in her bank account, and also had a very good idea of how much of a breathing space it would buy her from her father's persistent demands.

'I've decided to meet up with Marco this weekend,' Alejandro told her. 'I don't think he's going to speak to me of his own free will, but I did want to give him the opportunity to make the first approach.'

'Give him some more time,' Jemima suggested.

'I can't, *tesora mia*,' Alejandro countered, his lean, strong face shadowing. 'I have to deal with him. This feud has gone on long enough, though I can see that it suited Marco to keep us all at a distance. By the way, Beatriz knows.'

'I suspected that she might,' Jemima confided.

'She knew for a fact that Dario was gay and worked it out from there. But, being Beatriz, she said nothing to anyone for fear of causing offence,' Alejandro remarked wryly. 'I could wish she had been less scrupulous. Is it the prospect of my confronting Marco which is making you so jumpy?'

Jemima tensed, violet eyes veiling. 'Jumpy?'

'This past week I've often had the feeling that you're worrying about something. I assure you that I have no plans to have a huge messy row with my brother. It's a little late for that.'

Taken aback that he had noticed that she was living on her nerves, Jemima nodded and tried to look unconcerned.

'For the sake of the family I'll keep it under control, but I don't think I could ever forgive him for what he allowed me to believe,' he admitted squarely.

'Let it go with Marco. It's all in the past and over and done with,' Jemima pointed out just before she climbed out of the car outside the castle.

Alejandro closed a possessive arm round her on the stairs. The tangy scent of his citrus-based aftershave flared her nostrils and sent a flood of helpless awareness travelling to the more sensitive parts of her body. Unfortunately that was as close as he came to instigating a more intimate connection. Later she lay in bed about a foot away from him and wondered why he was still keeping his distance. Of course she could have bridged the gap, but why risk rocking the boat when she was already so stressed and feeling far from daring? Even during the night hours she was always somehow waiting for another phone call to destroy her peace of mind.

On the surface, though, most things were now fine in their marriage and she was determined to accept that without looking for pitfalls and pressures that might not exist. After all, her one and only real problem was Stephen Grey and what he might do. She told herself that if she continued to stand up to her father, he would eventually give up and leave her alone.

So, Alejandro had never said that he loved her and he probably never would, she reflected ruefully. Well, that was life. You couldn't have everything and what you did get was rarely perfect. He was making a real effort to make her happy and he was also proving to be a terrific father. It didn't get much better than that, she bargained with herself, determined not to succumb to taking for granted what she did have in favour of craving the one thing she couldn't have. She had always loved him, had learned to get by without him when their marriage failed, but now she was older and wiser and she knew that no other man could make her feel as good about herself or as happy as Alejandro did without even trying very hard.

In the week that followed it seemed to Jemima that Alejandro was angling at winning some 'perfect husband' award. Even though he disliked nightclubs, he took her out in Seville and they stayed over in the apartment there. They had a picnic down by the castle lake in the shelter of the trees with Alfie on what felt like the hottest day of the year and she paddled at the water's edge with her son chuckling in her arms. In the cool of the evening they dined out on the terrace, a practice that Doña Hortencia had once dismissed as too common and undignified to even be considered.

At a family party held at Alejandro's uncle's home on the occasion of his seventieth birthday, Marco and Dario put in an appearance as a couple and Doña Hortencia claimed that she was ill and left early, while everyone else pretended not to have noticed anything in the least bit unusual. Jemima was asked if she would do the flowers for a cousin's wedding and Marco let it be known that he and his partner were heading back to New York that weekend. Doña Hortencia was popularly held to be prostrate with relief at the news that the closet door could be closed again. Marco, on the other hand, informed Jemima that his mother had taken the news without comment; she was certainly annoyed with him but was still giving him his allowance. He also confessed that he was surprised by his older brother's continuing coolness towards him, an admission that made Dario Ortini, who was more sensitive, glance at Jemima in some embarrassment.

The next morning, Jemima was making some notes of her ideas for the flowers for the family wedding when Maria announced a visitor in an unusually anxious and apologetic tone.

Even while she was frowning in surprise at the sound of the housekeeper's strained voice, Jemima was truly appalled to scramble upright and see her father walking into the huge salon as bold as brass. While not tall, he was a broadly built man. With his shaven head and diamond ear studs, not to mention a purple and pink striped sports shirt, Stephen Grey was quite a sight to his daughter's dismayed eyes.

'This place is in the back of beyond. I had to pay a taxi a fortune to get up here!' he complained, sweeping the beautifully furnished room with assessing eyes that were striving to tot up the price of everything he could see. 'I hope you're planning to make coming out to Spain worth my while!'

Mastering her consternation at the older man's appearance, Jemima sucked in a deep steadying breath. She was grateful that Alejandro was out on the estate and unlikely to return before evening. 'What are you doing here? I asked you to leave me alone.'

His bloodshot blue eyes hardened. 'You've got no business talking to me like that, Jem!' he retorted furiously, his voice rising steeply. 'I brought you into the world and raised you and I expect you to treat me with proper respect.'

Jemima was very pale but she didn't back off, even though he was too close and too loud for comfort. 'After the way you treated me and my mother, I don't owe you the time of day,' she argued with an anger she couldn't hide. 'You washed your hands of me when I was only a teenager. My son and I have a good life here and I'm not about to let you ruin it for me.'

'Aw…will your fancy-pants Spanish Count be too much of a snob to keep you, once he knows what stock you're from?' Stephen Grey sneered, strolling over to the fireplace to lift a miniature portrait off the wall beside it and give the delicate gold and pearl-studded frame an intent scrutiny.

Alarm ran through Jemima as she watched. 'Please put that back. It's very old…'

The older man sent her a knowing look. 'It must be worth a packet on the antique market, then. If you can't help me with some cash like the last time, you can at least close your eyes while I help myself to a few little items that I can sell.'

'*No!*' Jemima shot back at him, crossing the pastel embroidered rug to stand in front of him. 'You can't have it. Give it back to me!'

The older man slid the portrait into his pocket and studied her with scorn. 'Mind your own business, why don't you? Either I take some stuff now or I come back some night with a few mates and we help ourselves to a good deal more.'

'If there's ever a burglary here, I will tell Alejandro about you.'

Stephen Grey loosed a derisive laugh. 'You won't! You'll do anything to keep that husband of yours in ignorance. You're the one who set a price on keeping the truth from him.'

'Yes, and I was very wrong. I understand that now,' Jemima conceded painfully. 'Now give me that miniature back before I call the police—'

'You wouldn't dare call the police!' he bit out with smug assurance.

In a complete panic because she was afraid that he might be right on that score and its potential for extreme embarrassment, Jemima tried to slide a hand into his pocket to retrieve the miniature portrait from him. He struck her shoulder with a big clenched fist to push her out of his way and she went flying off her feet and fell backwards across the coffee table. A startled yelp escaped her as she struck her head against a wooden chair leg and she lay in a heap, momentarily in a daze, one hand flying up to the bump at the back of her head.

There was a loud noise as the door burst open and then an outburst of strident Spanish. An instant later, Alejandro was lifting Jemima bodily up off the floor, settling her down with care on a sofa and demanding to know how she had got hurt.

'He's my father and he's threatening me,' Jemima whispered dizzily, way beyond trying to cover up the sordid scene and present it other than how it was. 'He has one of the portrait miniatures in his pocket and he hit me when I tried to get it back off him.'

'Now you listen 'ere,' her parent began loudly.

'The portrait first,' Alejandro murmured flatly, extending an authoritative hand.

Scowling, the older man dug the item out and passed it over. Blinking, her head pounding less from the blow she had sustained than from the thud of the unbearable tension, Jemima watched her husband return it to the wall. She saw her father lean close and say something to Alejandro and a split second later, and to her intense shock, Alejandro swung round and punched her father hard. The older man reeled back with a gasp of pain while Alejandro flung open the door and told him to get out before he brought the police in. Two vineyard workers were waiting outside and, at a word from Alejandro, they marched in and propelled Stephen Grey, struggling and vociferously complaining, out of the room.

'How on earth did you know what was happening in here?' Jemima demanded shakily.

'He frightened Maria by forcing his way in to see you. She didn't like the look of him or the way he spoke to her. I was at the vineyard and she phoned me immediately to warn me that there might be trouble.'

'I suppose you'll never forgive me now for not telling you the truth,' Jemima mumbled shakily as Alejandro sank down beside her to turn her head and gently examine the slight swelling at the back of her head. 'But when we first met I no longer had any contact with my father and I pretended he was dead rather than tell you about his history.'

Alejandro released his breath on a slow hiss. 'I think I can understand why.'

'He has a criminal record as long as your arm,' Jemima confided. And then she stopped trying to pick her words and the whole sorry story of her childhood came tumbling out: her father's violence and long stays in prison, her mother's alcoholism and the toxic atmosphere in their home.

'That you had found a decent job for yourself and were fully independent when we first met says much more about your character than the accident of birth that gave you your parents,' Alejandro told her with quiet confidence. 'I'm not stupid. I always knew that there were things you were choosing not to talk about and I wish I had dug deeper but it never seemed important enough to me. I wanted you as my wife whoever you were and regardless of what background you came from…'

Jemima looked at him through tear-filled eyes, her emotions swelling and overflowing in the aftermath of that nasty, distressing confrontation with her father. 'Honestly?'

'Walking away was never an option for me. I met you and that was that—it was a done deal. Do you remember the weekends we spent together at the house I rented near the hotel where you worked?' Alejandro queried, dark eyes intent on her troubled face as she nodded uncertainly. 'Those weekends were some of the happiest of my life and I could never have let you go after that.'

'But when we were first seeing each other you kept on breaking dates or not phoning when you said you would.'

Alejandro groaned. 'I regret the way I behaved but, right from the start, I was fighting what I felt for you. It was unnerving to want you so much. I wasn't ready to settle down. After what I'd suffered through my father's obsession with his second wife, I was determined not to fall in love either.'

'The differences between us bothered you.'

'Until I began to see that those differences meant that we complemented each other. After that month when we were broken up, when we were first dating, I knew just how necessary you were to my peace of mind,'

Alejandro admitted tautly, his lean, strong face grave. 'You were like no other woman I had ever met and I was fascinated.'

'I thought…' Jemima breathed in deep and went ahead and said it anyway. 'I thought that for you it was just sex.'

'Just sex would have been easier to deal with,' Alejandro quipped. 'I didn't know at the time that you were my soul mate, I only knew that I wanted you in my life every day and not just on the weekends I could travel to England. When I was away from you I missed you so much that the only option left was to make you my wife.'

'It didn't seem like that then. You never mentioned needing me that much.'

'Of course, I didn't, *preciosa mia*. I was trying to play it cool and I never will be into sharing my every waking thought,' he pointed out wryly. 'But the point is that I stopped seeing other women so that I could have you all to myself, and the more I saw of you, the more I wanted you to be mine. It's my fault that you didn't feel you could tell me about your background—obviously I didn't make you feel secure enough.'

'Even before I met you I was telling people when they asked that both my parents were dead—it was easier than telling the truth,' she admitted. 'That's where some of the money I ran through went two years ago. Dad was threatening to go to the newspapers and tell all to embarrass you.'

'It won't embarrass me. Let him do his worst if he must,' Alejandro responded with immense assurance. 'And don't be upset if he carries out his threats. Most people will only have a passing interest in the fact that your father is a jailbird. So, you allowed him to black-mail you when we were first married?'

'Yes. I thought you'd be ashamed of me if you found out the truth of the kind of home I was from. You'd have to go back a generation to find any respectable relatives.'

Alejandro closed two hands over hers and held her fast. 'I just wish that you'd told me that you were being threatened and that you'd given me the chance to sort him out for you. Your father is like most bullies—once he saw that I wasn't afraid of him or what he might do, he was weak.'

'You must hate me, though, for giving all that money to him and wasting it,' Jemima reasoned, pale with shame and discomfiture.

'You were foolish. You could have trusted me even then.' Alejandro gazed down at her with dark eyes filled with regret. 'But I do appreciate that I wasn't a good enough husband in those days to inspire you with that trust. Without it, you were lost and your father got a stranglehold on you instead.'

'He's the other reason why I walked out then,' Jemima confided abruptly. 'It wasn't just your suspicions about my relationship with Marco, it was the fact that I also couldn't see an end to my father's demands for money. I just felt our marriage was cursed and that the best thing I could do was walk away from it.'

'The best thing you could have done was confide in me. I wouldn't let anyone harm you ever again,' Alejandro swore with conviction. 'But I made too much of a habit of feeling and thinking things that I didn't then share with you and that's one very good reason why our marriage broke down.'

Jemima looked up into his somber, darkly handsome face and stretched up to kiss him. For an instant he stiffened and then he kissed her back with such passionate fervour that she gasped beneath the onslaught. Her heart thumping like a piston, she pressed her hot face against his shoulder and struggled to catch her breath again. 'I was starting to think that you were never going to kiss me again.'

'I was playing safe by making no demands.'

Jemima looked blank. 'What on earth are you talking about?'

'Our agreement that we give our marriage a three-month trial,' Alejandro reminded her grimly. 'The three months were up this week and there you were acting strangely. Naturally, I thought that you were on edge because you were thinking of leaving me again and were worrying about how to go about it and retain custody of Alfie.'

Jemima was frowning. 'My word, I totally forgot about the three-month thing!'

'You *forgot*?' Alejandro exclaimed with incredulous emphasis. 'How could you forget an agreement like that? It's been haunting me ever since I was stupid enough to say yes to it.'

'Oh, so that's why you took me dancing,' Jemima guessed with a sudden giggle of appreciation.

'I got so much wrong in my relationship with you I had to make an effort to get some things right,' Alejandro pointed out darkly, his dignity clearly under threat from her growing amusement. 'I was scared that you had decided to return to England.'

Jemima rested a hand on his shirtfront, spreading her fingers to feel the solid pound of his heart and the heat of his muscular torso through the fine cotton. 'I want you for ever,' she told him without hesitation.

His hand covered hers. 'For ever?' he questioned with a frown.

'Like the castle in the fairy tale. For ever and ever... I'm greedy, I want it *all*.'

'All I want is you,' Alejandro confided in a roughened undertone. 'All I've ever wanted is you. I love you very much.'

Her heart leapt but so did her eyebrows. 'Since when?' she asked, initially suspicious of the claim.

'Since very soon after I met you, only I didn't want to admit it even to myself because it made me feel so powerless, *querida*,' he confided heavily.

'But you never told me that you loved me then.'

'I was stingy with the words,' Alejandro admitted ruefully. 'But why do you think I married you? We were dynamite in bed together, but I wouldn't have married you if I hadn't felt a great deal more for you. I was crushed when you walked out on our marriage.'

'Maybe it was for the best.' Jemima sighed, her violet eyes pools of deep reflective emotion. 'I needed to grow up a lot. I was too immature for you.'

'I knew you were too young to get married, but I couldn't face waiting any longer for you. I wouldn't even wait long enough for my stepmother to organise a wedding for us,' he pointed out.

'I didn't even know that that was ever an option.'

'It wasn't once I realised how long the arrangements would take. I was counting the days until I could bring you back to Spain. That's why I opted for a quick ceremony in England.'

For the first time she began believing in what he was

telling her and a wondering smile lit up her face. 'We rushed into getting married…'

'But with the very best of intentions,' he traded. 'Don't ever walk out on me again.'

'I won't.' Jemima hesitated as a long-suppressed thought occurred to her and then spoke up. 'After I left were there other women…affairs?'

'No. I told myself I would wait until I was divorced,' Alejandro extended. 'But I didn't want anyone else. I still wanted you.'

'There wasn't anyone else for me either,' Jemima volunteered.

He framed her cheekbones with long brown fingers and regarded her intently. 'Don't ever leave me again.'

'I'm not going anywhere,' she declared, and then she blushed. 'Apart from, well, if you should feel like it, our bedroom.'

It took a moment for Alejandro to grasp that invitation and then he wasted no time in vaulting upright and grasping her hand. 'Shouldn't I take you to a doctor to get that bruise on your head checked?'

'It's a bump and I saw stars for an instant, that's all. What I *really* want…'

'I'm more than ready to give you, *preciosa mia*,' Alejandro intoned with raging enthusiasm, pausing only to bundle her into his arms and mount the stairs with her clasped to his chest like a valued gift.

But Jessica had yet to forgive him for those nights she had lain awake wondering. 'I was worried that, maybe, as far as you were concerned, the passion had gone off the boil…'

'I'm on the boil round the clock!' Alejandro contradicted with a feeling groan, shouldering open the bedroom door and tumbling her down on the bed with an impressive amount of energy. 'I always want you.'

And he discarded her clothes and his in an untidy heap while he stole hot, hungry kisses from her willing mouth. His hands found her swollen breasts, the tender peaks and the moist heat between her legs. Seconds later he plunged into her and the intensity of her response hit fever pitch. Her orgasm roared up through her like an unstoppable fountain of burning sparks. She came apart in his arms, crying out her wild hot pleasure.

'Is this the optimum moment to tell you that I forgot to use a condom, *mi corazón*?' Alejandro drawled, his chest rising and falling rapidly as he struggled to catch his breath in the aftermath.

Jemima froze, thought about the possible consequences and then gave him a great big sunny smile because he had called her, 'my heart'. 'I suppose it must be because I forgot as well.'

'I would love to have another baby with you,' Alejandro husked, his dark golden eyes full of tenderness as he kissed her and held her close with possessive arms. 'I would like it very much indeed.'

'We could always try.'

Alejandro lifted his dark head and looked down at her with a heart stopping grin that made her feel all warm and squashy inside. 'I would like trying to get you pregnant very much as well, *preciosa mia*.'

'And if at first you don't succeed, try, try again,' Jemima reminded him with dancing eyes of amusement.

'That strikes me as the perfect blueprint for a second honeymoon. We'll go to the coast—Alfie will love the beach,' Alejandro forecast with satisfaction.

'I love you, Alejandro Navarro Vasquez,' Jemima told him, hugging him tightly to her.

'But not as much as I love you, *mi vide,*' Alejandro countered. 'You and Alfie are my whole world. Without you I would have nothing.'

Afloat on a wonderful cloud of happy contentment with all her worries and fears laid to rest, Jemima kissed him with tender loving appreciation.

A year later, Jemima gave birth to her daughter, Candice, a blue-eyed, black-haired little darling, who charmed both her parents and her big brother long before she gave them her first smile.

Jemima had sold her florist's shop in the village of Charlbury St Helens and had decided against opening a similar business in Spain because to make it a viable full-time enterprise she would have had to base it in Seville. Besides, decorating houses with flowers was less of a tradition in her adopted country. She did act as a floral consultant for several smart weddings and events in the extended family circle and once she learned that she was carrying her second child she was no longer concerned about how she would fill her time. Her fear that her pregnancy would be as difficult as the first proved unfounded and she suffered very little sickness and, when the time came, enjoyed a straightforward delivery. Raising her children, acting as Alejandro's hostess when they entertained at the castle, and continuing to take a strong interest in the charity that supported the women's shelter and enshrined the cause of battered women kept Jemima more than sufficiently busy.

Flora flew out every three months or so for a visit. Beatriz met an architect at a family christening and was married to him within six months. Currently expecting her first child, Beatriz was a good deal more confident than she had once been and remained Jemima's closest friend in Spain. Of all of them, Doña Hortencia had changed the least. Although Marco still visited his mother, relations were often strained between them because it remained a challenge for her to accept him as he was. On the other hand, her strong desire to retain her ties with the castle had ensured that the older woman had become much more polite to Jemima.

Alejandro and Marco had repaired their brotherly bond to some extent but past history ensured that Alejandro remained wary. Marco, however, was flourishing at the art gallery in New York and, having found his true métier, was steadily climbing the career ladder. In the field of business, the brothers shared a very strong bond indeed.

Alfie was thriving and had recently started preschool, which was improving his grasp of Spanish by leaps and bounds. Stephen Grey had sold a story about his wealthy daughter and son-in-law to a downmarket British tabloid but the article hadn't amounted to much and had attracted little attention. Since then Jemima had heard nothing from her father, although Alejandro had established that the older man had recently lost his freedom, having been returned to jail for committing an offence.

Jemima remained exuberantly happy with her life and never allowed herself to forget how close she had come to losing Alejandro and the marriage that had become the centre of her world. She told him just about everything and hid almost nothing from him and, in turn, he tried to talk more to her and share his deeper concerns. If he was working very long hours, Jemima stayed in Seville so that they saw more of each other. With a little compromise and mutual respect on both sides, they had ensured that they were closer than ever by the time that they celebrated the first anniversary of their reconciliation with a holiday in England.

Three months on from that, Jemima was in the Seville apartment, awaiting the sound of Alejandro's key in the lock on the front door. When she heard it, she flew out of bed and raced out to the hall, a slight figure in a black silk nightdress.

Alejandro leant back against the door to shut it, all the while studying her with appreciative dark golden eyes and a charismatic smile that made her tummy flip. 'You make coming home such an event, *esposa mia*,' he told her huskily.

'You've already eaten, haven't you?' she checked, moving forward to trail his jacket off his shoulders and lock flirtatious fingers round his tie to ease it slowly out from below his collar.

'I ordered in food once I knew that the talks would run late.' Keen to be of help, Alejandro jerked his shirt out of the waistband of his trousers and kicked off his shoes. He knew their housekeeper would find a trail of clothes leading down to the bedroom in the morning but he didn't care. He was delighted when his wife pounced on him. His shirt drifted down to the floor.

Jemima settled big violet eyes on his superb bronzed torso and uttered an appreciative sigh, which made him feel ten feet tall. On the threshold of the bedroom, he stepped out of his trousers and a step later paused to shed his socks.

'I really love being married to you,' Alejandro confessed raggedly as he came down on the bed.

Surveying Alejandro in his boxer shorts, Jemima had no complaints to make either. Indeed she was dizzily conscious of the sheer happiness bubbling through her. 'I love you too—more every day…'

He leant forward and kissed her and she quivered with pleasure and anticipation, revelling in the reality that it was a Friday and they had the whole night to enjoy each other. Much as they loved Alfie, it would be relaxing not to have a lively toddler sneaking into their bed at first light and ensuring that any fun had to be clean fun. The pressure of her handsome husband's mouth on hers was unbearably sexy.

'I love you…more than I have words to describe,' Alejandro told her thickly.

'I've got plenty of words,' she broke free to tell him.

'Shush,' he urged, kissing her again until she forgot what she had been talking about and settled up against his lean powerful body like an extra layer of skin. The silence that ensued was broken only by revealing little gasps, moans and sighs while Alfie and Candice's parents got thoroughly acquainted again after a day spent apart…

Things are heating up...

For three couples, this weekend will
be unforgettable, incredible and
completely mind-blowing!

Available 7th January 2011

MODERN

HIDDEN MISTRESS, PUBLIC WIFE
by Emma Darcy

Women fall at billionaire Jordan Powell's feet, so the challenge of seducing farm girl Ivy Thornton is a diverting amusement. But Ivy isn't prepared to be another disposable mistress…

THE FORBIDDEN INNOCENT
by Sharon Kendrick

Ashley Jones desperately needs her new job as formidable author Jack Marchant's assistant. Her heart goes out to her tortured boss—then one day they begin an affair that is as secret as it is forbidden…

THE SECRETARY'S SCANDALOUS SECRET
by Cathy Williams

When Luc Loughton discovers Agatha Havers' tantalising curves, awakening his wholesome secretary goes to the top of his agenda! Agatha is living the fairytale—until she's brought back to reality with a bump…

PRINCE VORONOV'S VIRGIN
by Lynn Raye Harris

Paige Barnes is rescued from the dark streets of Moscow by Prince Alexei Voronov—her boss's deadliest rival. Now he has Paige unexpectedly in his sights, Alexei will play emotional Russian roulette to keep her close…

On sale from 17th December 2010
Don't miss out!

Available at WHSmith, Tesco, ASDA, Eason
and all good bookshops
www.millsandboon.co.uk

MODERN

JORDAN ST CLAIRE: DARK AND DANGEROUS
by Carole Mortimer

Helping aristocratic actor Jordan St Claire recuperate from an accident, physiotherapist Stephanie McKinley discovers the man behind the famous façade…and he's determined to unleash her reserved sensuality!

BOUND TO THE GREEK
by Kate Hewitt

Greek tycoon Jace Zervas hires Eleanor Langley—the flame he extinguished years ago—purely for business. But, secluded under the hot Mediterranean sun, Jace finds the fire of passion still burns…

RUTHLESS BOSS, DREAM BABY
by Susan Stephens

Magenta isn't expecting the old-fashioned ruthlessness of her new boss Gray Quinn! He'll give her the night of her life, but he might not be there when she wakes up… And he definitely doesn't want her taking maternity leave!

MISTRESS, MOTHER…WIFE?
by Maggie Cox

Dante Romano has fought hard to get where he is today—but nothing compares to discovering he's the father of a child. Marrying Anna Bailey is the only option to right the wrongs of the past…so he'll see her at the altar, willing or not…

On sale from 7th January 2011
Don't miss out!

Available at WHSmith, Tesco, ASDA, Eason and all good bookshops

www.millsandboon.co.uk

With This Fling...
by Kelly Hunter
Charlotte Greenstone's convenient, fictional fiancé *inconveniently* resembles sexy stranger Greyson Tyler! Grey agrees to keep Charlotte's secret as long as they enjoy *all* the benefits of a real couple...

Girls' Guide to Flirting with Danger
by Kimberly Lang
When the media discover that marriage counsellor Megan Lowe is the ex-wife of an infamous divorce attorney, Megan has to take the plunge and face her dangerously sexy ex.

Juggling Briefcase & Baby
by Jessica Hart
A weekend working with his ex, Romy, and her baby, Freya, has corporate genius Lex confused. Opposites they may be, but Lex's attraction to happy-go-lucky Romy seems to have grown stronger with the years...

Deserted Island, Dreamy Ex
by Nicola Marsh
Starring in an island-based TV show sounded blissful, until Kristi discovered her Man Friday was her ex, Jared Malone. Of course, she doesn't feel *anything* for him, but can't help hoping he'll like her new bikini...

On sale from 3rd December 2010
Don't miss out!

Available at WHSmith, Tesco, ASDA, Eason and all good bookshops

www.millsandboon.co.uk

2 FREE BOOKS
AND A SURPRISE GIFT

We would like to take this opportunity to thank you for reading this Mills & Boon® book by offering you the chance to take TWO more specially selected books from the Modern™ series absolutely FREE! We're also making this offer to introduce you to the benefits of the Mills & Boon® Book Club™—

- **FREE home delivery**
- **FREE gifts and competitions**
- **FREE monthly Newsletter**
- **Exclusive Mills & Boon Book Club offers**
- **Books available before they're in the shops**

Accepting these FREE books and gift places you under no obligation to buy, you may cancel at any time, even after receiving your free books. Simply complete your details below and return the entire page to the address below. You don't even need a stamp!

YES Please send me 2 free Modern books and a surprise gift. I understand that unless you hear from me, I will receive 4 superb new books every month for just £3.30 each, postage and packing free. I am under no obligation to purchase any books and may cancel my subscription at any time. The free books and gift will be mine to keep in any case.

Ms/Mrs/Miss/Mr _____ Initials _____

Surname _____

Address _____

_____ Postcode _____

E-mail _____

Send this whole page to: Mills & Boon Book Club, Free Book Offer, FREEPOST NAT 10298, Richmond, TW9 1BR

Offer valid in UK only and is not available to current Mills & Boon Book Club subscribers to this series. Overseas and Eire please write for details.. We reserve the right to refuse an application and applicants must be aged 18 years or over. Only one application per household. Terms and prices subject to change without notice. Offer expires 28th February 2011. As a result of this application, you may receive offers from Harlequin Mills & Boon and other carefully selected companies. If you would prefer not to share in this opportunity please write to The Data Manager, PO Box 676, Richmond, TW9 1WU.

Mills & Boon® is a registered trademark owned by Harlequin Mills & Boon Limited.
Modern™ is being used as a trademark. The Mills & Boon® Book Club™ is being used as a trademark.